"We've got to take them out."

Barrabas had spoken in deadly undertones. Manuel nodded in response, and they moved stealthily toward the sentries on the beach.

A *whoosh* indicated that vital oxygen had been released from the air tanks. Though the diving gear had been well concealed, the sentries had stumbled upon it and were even now in heated argument, unaware of the shadows looming over them.

An alarm would be raised any minute, cutting off the hope of escape. There was no time to waste. Shoving off from the small rise just above the sentries' position, Barrabas and Manuel sailed through the air in unison, their glinting knives stretched before them like the claws of predators.

SOLDIERS OF BARRABAS

SOLDIERS OF BARRABAS

THE BARRABAS CREED

JACK HILD

A GOLD EAGLE BOOK FROM

WORLDWIDE.

TORONTO · NEW YORK · LONDON · PARIS
AMSTERDAM · STOCKHOLM · HAMBURG
ATHENS · MILAN · TOKYO · SYDNEY

First edition May 1988

ISBN 0-373-61624-4

Special thanks and acknowledgment to
John Preston for his contribution to this work.

1

"What the hell could it have been?" Chief Inspector Ole Ericson said with bewilderment, casting one more aghast glance at the group of blood-spattered bodies sprawled on the pavement. It sounded like a demand of the other officers of the Intelligence Division of the Swedish police to come up with an answer right there on the scene of the assassination. "What could possibly be going on that the prime minister of a neutral country, his wife and his bodyguard are all dead?"

No one had an answer. Their inability to respond was made all the worse by their shared knowledge that the chief inspector's question was going to be echoed forcefully by every newspaper in the kingdom, every politician in the parliament and the whole body of citizenry.

Implicit in the query was another question all those interrogators would want to have answered: how could they—the men of the intelligence division—have allowed it to happen?

The assassination of the prime minister of Sweden was a dark moment in Swedish history. The gruesome evidence that their country was vulnerable to the violence that was so commonplace elsewhere was something that shocked Swedes. Their country had passed the last hurdle into the center ring of world affairs, it seemed, and was on the one stage that no one wanted to occupy. And the spotlight was unblinkingly fixed on the unresponsive limp corpses that looked so unremarkable, so much like ordinary citizens even in death. But a certain grotesque twist to the limbs, the torsos, spoke of an undeserved visitation of violence into that peaceful country and those almost ordinary lives. The blood transfixed the horror, the shock, the shattered illusion of peace in a pain-racked world.

"It was a 9 mm slug, Chief Inspector," one of the attending detectives reported. "A Beretta, perhaps, or just as possibly one of the new Brazilian copies—a Llama or a Taurus."

"Yes, yes," Ericson acknowledged impatiently, dismissing the evidence. The Brazilian automatic pistol with its 18-round capability had become one of the favorite weapons among police forces around the world. Even the Americans were importing the damn things for their police departments, enraging civil libertarians because the eighteen rounds represented massive firepower, they claimed, much too much for the needs of civilian restraint. What those do-gooders never seemed to remember was that the criminals in the world had just as easy access to the Llamas and the Tauruses, Ericson summed up the situation in his mind. The Brazilians, in their newfound role as major international arms exporters, weren't noted for their discretion in choosing their customers.

That was all they needed, Ericson realized when he thought through that report on the weapon. An unidentifiable weapon in the hands of an unidentifiable assailant. They hadn't come up with a single witness to the assault, or even one who could say that there had been any unusual characters in the vicinity.

"Bergson!" Ericson called out to the officer who was standing on the periphery of the circle of agents. "Weren't you supposed to be on duty tonight?"

"I switched with Johanson, sir. It was a celebration. We went through the channels—"

"Yes, yes," Ericson said, deflecting the stream of self-justification that he was sure his underling was ready to unleash on him. "I'm sure you did it right. Lucky for you." The chief inspector looked at the dead male body on the stones in front of him. "Damned lucky."

"Yes, sir, very lucky indeed," Bergson said, glad he had a couple of double Scotches under his belt to help him hide the knowing look that was trying to creep across his face. He tuned out as the ambulances arrived and carted the bodies away, and he replayed the evening in his mind, using the dead woman's comments that had drifted within earshot to imagine the scene as she must have seen it happen to her. There was a certain satisfaction to this, he thought....

"THIS COULD ONLY HAPPEN in a country like ours."

In response, Christina Malstrom looked over at her husband's self-satisfied expression. "What do you mean, darling?"

"That the prime minister of Sweden and his lovely wife can take a stroll through the streets of the capital city on a pleasant summer evening, the same as any other happily married couple. We haven't the crowds of rowdy tourists who follow the British leaders, or the intrusive, combative journalists who monitor every waking moment of the American politicians. We are simply a pleasantly middle-aged pair taking a walk through Stockholm."

"Middle-aged!" Christina scoffed. "Speak for yourself, old man."

Sven Malstrom turned and grinned at his wife. "You are quite right; I am the one who is old and decrepit. You are young and beautiful."

"Or I was that twenty years ago."

Their bantering was good-natured fun. They had had variations of the conversation many times and in many different circumstances as their lives and careers had progressed. The recognition made Christina think back over the twenty years she'd been married to Sven, long before they had become the prime minister and his lady.

They had started out at Uppsala, the university that was the crown of the Swedish educational establishment. They had been devoted idealists then. Actually, she realized with a smile, they were still that now. Idealism was possibly a rare commodity in the modern world, but it still had its place in Sweden, at least.

And Sven was right. Theirs was one of the few countries in the world where the head of government could walk city streets without concern. Sweden didn't have the terrorist problems that plagued the rest of Western Europe, and it certainly wasn't a dictatorship with disgruntled lower classes that would want to attack a symbol of the state out of rage and frustration.

"Still, darling, it's not as though we are really simple citizens of the state without any of the trappings of privilege," Christina said.

"What do you mean?" Sven asked.

Christina nodded back at the two plainclothes Swedish policemen who were trailing them.

"Window dressing," Sven said dismissively.

"So, do we really live in a society without any problems?"

"Of course not," Sven said.

Christina was immediately sorry she'd brought up the subject. She saw a cloud come over her husband's face. Her innocent remark had obviously brought up some unpleasant subject.

"Sven, what is it?"

They were walking through the old part of Stockholm, on the narrow streets near the ancient Town Hall that had been the center of the city for centuries. The smells of the Baltic weren't far away, and the summer evening had been quiet since the city traffic had disappeared with nightfall. They weren't in one of the sections of town famous for nightlife, so there wasn't that noise and bustle to bother them. Stockholm was in its most pure, most pristine state, true to form as the city they'd fallen in love with when they'd moved to the capital from Uppsala to make their fortunes.

Apparently Sven wasn't in any mood to take notice of the simple pleasures around him. Christina was used to her husband's ability to leave behind the pressures of the state when they were alone together, but for once that talent was obviously failing him.

"It's..." Sven had been about to start a conversation that was obviously going to be difficult, but had stopped himself. "Darling, let's not. It's just something that's come out of the Gustavus Adolphus Institute. It's complex and bothersome, and I really would like to have a vacation from it, even if just for this evening."

Christina knew when not to press her husband and recognized that it was one of those times. It wasn't easy, though. The name of the most prestigious and famous chemical laboratory in Scandinavia wasn't something to make a soul free at ease. Swedes—like the Americans—have a fascination with technological progress. Until recently, both people had assumed that whatever came out of research had to be good.

Chernobyl was only one of many incidents to challenge that belief. Increasingly, it seemed to many that science now threatened to produce new plagues for Western society, and ultimately, the world.

So many terrors had been unthinkingly unleashed on the world by experiments gone wrong, or as unexpected side effects of seemingly beneficial "advances." Christina shuddered as she remembered the report made by the Minister of the Environment at a Cabinet dinner party only recently.

It seemed that fluorocarbons were suspected of eating away at the earth's ozone layer with appalling efficiency. There was real danger, the minister had warned, if Western societies weren't willing to cut down on their use, and do it soon. The ozone layer the chemicals were guilty of eroding was made up of a form of oxygen in the stratosphere that limited the amount of ultraviolet rays penetrating the earth atmosphere. Without that protective layer, skin cancer was potentially going to become epidemic among humans, and the effect on plant life could only be guessed at.

Fluorocarbons! To Christina and most of the rest of the world, those chemical compounds were nothing more than modern conveniences performing such innocuous tasks as propelling whipped cream from canisters. Now fluorocarbons were implicated in endangering human life as they left the planet with less and less defense against potentially lethal rays from the sun.

If that could be such a problem, what could be going on in Sven's mind that was worrying him even more? She didn't even want to think about it.

The annoyance of the intrusion of Sven's unnamed worry made Christina edgy. Perhaps the prime minister of Sweden had fewer pressures in his life than did his counterparts in other countries qualifying as industrial giants, but the fact couldn't be denied that Sven had been under tremendous strain lately. Christina didn't like it, not one bit.

She willed herself to smile and continue with their walk, deciding that the last thing Sven needed then was a worried wife to add to his anxiety.

But she did wish the policemen weren't with them. There were times when she wanted to do something utterly outrageous as a reminder that she and her husband were human beings who enjoyed some play by themselves. She'd imagined the expressions on the guards' faces if they could see the revered prime minister and his lady naked in their bedroom, recreating one of their intimate bedroom fantasies.

Following up her thoughts, she automatically turned slightly toward the pair following them on one of the small dark alleyways so common in that part of the city. She saw the quiet one reach inside his jacket to retrieve something. What was his name? she wondered quickly. He was one of the faceless many who shadowed them through their lives.

She had just barely remembered that he was Bergson when she saw a pistol in his hand, obviously what he had been reaching for. What could be the problem? she thought with a quiver of apprehension. She immediately knew it was ridiculous to take stock of the gun with a kind of revulsed curiosity. She had no knowledge of arms and couldn't have identified the weapon, but she did notice the unusual length of the long barrel. She'd seen something like that in a movie once, she thought, when the pistol had a silencer to muffle its sound. The realization hit home.

"Sven!" she gasped. Christina had tried to scream out her husband's name, but her voice seemed to strangle on itself. The silencer was the element that had made her acutely aware of the danger. She wanted to alert her husband, but just wasn't able to yell as her throat constricted with fear. Her warning escaped from her mouth as a raspy whisper instead.

"Darling?" Malstrom turned toward his wife questioningly, not sure what her tone of voice implied.

Before she could say anything more, Christina saw Bergson aim the pistol at his partner. She felt a momentary relief that they weren't the man's target, but she instantly knew the comfort had been misplaced. The shot exploded with a strangely dulled sound, making the second policeman freeze in seeming shock. The bullet entered the back of his skull and then burst out the front, directly in the center of his forehead. Christina thought the exit wound was strangely large, but still so small, when one remembered that it had murdered the human being who had been standing there only seconds earlier.

"Oh, my God!" The expression came out of Christina in a whisper but inside it definitely was a scream. Every one of her nerve endings called out in panic and dread. She looked around madly, trying to find an escape, trying to find—

That same muted explosion sounded again, and there was a sudden heavy weight falling against her side. Christina put up her hand in a dazed manner to fend it off and felt a warm sticky fluid on her palm. She recoiled, letting Sven's body collapse onto the alley's cobblestones.

Now she did scream, for herself, for her husband, in fear, in anger, in vain.

There was a sudden sharp pain in her right breast that seemed to be accompanied by another weight pushing against her. But the weight was pressing against such a small area of her torso. Then there was the horrible sound of the muzzled gun again, and more pain and more pressure on her left side.

Then she experienced a strange falling sensation as she seemed to float downward and gracefully drape her body over her husband's. She was protecting Sven, she told herself. She was protecting her husband to the last.

And then she died.

Christina wasn't aware of the commotion that followed her death and didn't see Bergson hurriedly run to the end of the alley and motion madly with his hands.

As soon as he had, a trio of men appeared, two of them dragging a third between them. The third man appeared to be unconscious, and his weight was slowing them down and forced the two carriers to swear under their breath at the difficulty. As soon as the human cargo had been deposited near the three corpses, Bergson put his pistol to the man's head and shot him.

The four corpses were now piled in the narrow space, their blood mingling on the stones of ancient Stockholm.

2

COLONEL BUZZ MCDONOUGH thought that the man was a nerd. Buzz squirmed on his seat in the small lecture hall in the headquarters building of the United States Army Southern Command in Panama. He was a soldier, for God's sake! What was he doing listening to some research egghead from the Department of Agriculture talking about the soil conditions of the Amazon Basin?

Buzz had to make himself sit up in his chair to ensure that he didn't let the idiot lull him to sleep. He reminded himself that he should provide the other, more junior officers in the room with a role model. It wasn't easy, though. He had to force himself to pay attention to the academic's words.

"The first impression most North Americans have of the rain forest is one that is tinged with awe. We're conditioned by our observations of our own continent, and we assume that any soil that can support the lush tropical growth of the jungles must be so rich that it could sustain unlimited crop cultivation.

"For centuries, northern farmers coming to South America have looked at the rain forests and have believed that they have discovered a treasure as valuable as the fabled gold of the Incas.

"In every case, they've been wrong.

"The Chapare in Bolivia is a tributary of the Amazon, and the land it drains is also a part of the Amazon Basin.

This area, too, has held out the false promise of wealth and fortune to countless settlers. The truth of the matter is that, like the rest of the basin, the Chapare's soil is nearly worthless for commercial agriculture.

"It's important for you to understand the discrepancy between what we see and what actually exists in this area, if you're going to understand the problem you're up against."

The agriculture specialist went to the blackboard and began to draw charts. Buzz felt as though he were back in Miss Pritchard's class in eighth grade in Eau Claire, Wisconsin. He moaned, so frustrated by the flashback to his early adolescence that the sounds he was making came out much louder than he intended.

But one thing was different from the days in Miss Pritchard's class: Buzz was now a colonel in the United States Army. No one—not even the person at the head of the class—was going to dare to turn around and demand he offer up his palm for a whack with a ruler.

The scientist went on with his lecture, ignoring the sound from the class. He did, though, seem to become even more condescending, his own means of revenge on the unappreciative audience in front of which he had to perform.

"Our preconceived notions about the richness of the soil come from our own experiences with forests, as I already indicated. In North America, most of our trees shed their leaves with every season. Even our evergreens and other conifers regularly shed their needles—if not on a seasonal basis—as well as their cones or other seeds.

"This means that the trees are constantly enriching the earth. The material they let down onto the ground becomes a natural compost. Its nutrients enter into the earth, and the minerals and other elements are reabsorbed into the soil and are available to encourage new plants, or to sustain the old ones.

"Also, in North America, many of our trees have deep roots. They burrow many feet beneath the surface, breaking up the earth and aerating it.

"In the Chapare, these things don't happen. The equatorial climate never leads the growth into a cycle of death and rejuvenation. The trees simply continue to grow. The roots of the most common plants are also designed to spread outward rather than downward, and so the earth beneath a painfully shallow level of topsoil never becomes an accessible part of the—"

"What the hell does this have to do with shooting up drug dealers?"

Buzz looked over at Mike Hamson and smiled. As usual, the impetuous lieutenant was the first one to lose his cool.

Hamson was the kind of guy whom Buzz liked. The youngster had only just graduated from West Point—he actually had the good sense to seem embarrassed that he'd only left the academy so recently—and he was anxious to see some action. Being sent back into a classroom so quickly must have really galled the kid.

But Buzz had to say something to calm down the frowning captain from Army Intelligence who was standing in the corner at the front of the room. "Lieutenant, good intelligence is the cornerstone of good strategy."

"Yes, sir." Mike Hamson's reluctant response wasn't any more convincing than Buzz's reprimand had been.

The scientist seemed to hesitate for an extra minute before continuing. His silent reproach reminded Buzz all the more of Miss Pritchard, the old sourpuss.

"The fact is, the soil of the Amazon Basin in general and, in particular, of the Chapare, simply can't sustain full agricultural development. One of the very few crops capable of surviving in the region—once it's been cleared of the rain forest—is the coca plant, which is a particularly hardy bushy growth, something similar in its resilience to the scrub oak and scrub pine flourishing in our coastal beach areas, for instance.''

The scientist faced his audience squarely to make his final point. ''That, gentlemen, is the economic reality of your problem. The peasants aren't growing other crops because, quite simply, they couldn't survive if they did.''

That was apparently the end of the lecture. Finally, Buzz thought. The scientist sat down, and Captain Peterson, the man from Intelligence, took center stage.

Like every other man present, Buzz knew that the intelligence staff was not only directed to provide background information for an Army project such as the upcoming campaign in Bolivia, but it was also responsible for internal investigations. Yeah, Buzz reminded himself mentally, if you get your ass in grass, this is the son of a bitch who will tie it up, put a ribbon on it and hand it to the Joint Chiefs.

It wasn't something to make any representative beloved by the commanders in the field and often earned the unflattering classification of ''creep'' from them.

''To answer your question, Lieutenant,'' the intelligence captain began with a judgmental and threatening look directed at Mike Hamson, ''it has a great deal to do with your operation.

''United States policy had been operating under a misconception about the facts of life in Bolivia. We thought that the peasants had been growing coca under duress. We'd seen enough evidence of the kinds of pressure criminal elements can bring to bear on innocent people that we assumed something similar was going on here.

''We assumed that any peasant growing coca was an unwilling pawn of the criminal conspiracy. That's wrong. It's apparent now that the peasants are growing coca because it's the only crop from which they can make a living.

"As a result of our new understanding, Congress has decided to pay the peasants to relocate—" the captain broke off abruptly as the audience of career Army officers groaned in disgust at the idea.

"You mean we're going to throw millions of dollars at the Bolivians to try to pay off another one of our problems? When will Washington ever learn?"

The intelligence officer shot another look at Mike Hamson. It was a clear order for the young lieutenant to shut up. Mike grimaced with displeasure, but he did stop talking. Buzz felt even more empathy with the kid.

"The United States Army is not in the business of deciding foreign policy, but of carrying out its orders. Now, let's get back to the matter at hand.

"Our previous sorties into Bolivia have been misdirected. We attacked the growers and their crops as though they were enemies. The result was a public relations disaster that created an even more unstable situation in La Paz, the Bolivian capital. We unwittingly helped to undermine the central government by antagonizing its constituents among the peasantry in Chapare.

"This time, we're going to another source. Our orders are to assume the role of advisers to detachments of the Bolivian army and federal police...."

A communal round of snorts and guffaws made its way through the audience. Peterson chose to ignore the widespread rebellion and kept on talking. "But we're under firm orders to deal only with the factories where the coca leaves are turned into distilled cocaine.

"The factories are simply constructed, and their machinery is often primitive. A dangerous procedure involving hydrochloride and other volatile chemicals transforms the coca leaves into an easily transportable material. The pure cocaine is cut with inert ingredients to increase its bulk and for more profitable sale, something that's usually done in the Caribbean, though it's sometimes done once again in the United States to increase profits still more.

"In order to disrupt the flow of cocaine and other drugs into the continental states, we have got to go to the source—to Bolivia. That's your job. But American policy no longer sees the peasants as the enemies we once thought they were. They're innocents who've been trapped by economic forces; they're only pawns in this game.

"Our objectives in Operation Manufacture are the distilleries. We had, in the past, hoped for aid and encouragement from the peasants whom we had expected to treat us as liberators from the criminal forces overseeing them. We were wrong.

"But now the peasants have begun to see substantial amounts of the American aid reach their own pocketbooks. We don't expect them to oppose us. They still may not view us as liberators, but we expect to be viewed as the representatives of a benevolent power."

Does this guy really belive this bull? Buzz wondered to himself.

BUZZ SAT with Mike Hamson that night over a couple beers in a local bar in the zone.

The Panama Canal Zone was a bit of America set down in the middle of Central America. Just as the British had reconstructed their domestic life-style in their empire, the United States had fabricated a fake Middle America on the isthmus.

Buzz looked affectionately at Hamson and thought of himself years ago, fresh out of the academy, ready to go and save the world, or at least the United States Army.

McDonough was a lifer. He'd been in the Army for fifteen years already, with little expectation that he'd be one of those who ran for civilian life and a fat pension check the minute he hit the twenty-year mark. Being a soldier was the thing that made Buzz's life work because it gave a sense of purpose he just couldn't imagine if he were back in Wisconsin selling cars with his father-in-law.

"Mike, you really let those guys get to you today. Was it the politics that was bothering you?"

Hamson studied the dying head of foam on his beer and slowly shook his head. "Nah. I expect politics to get fouled up in anything like this, I don't care about that: I care about the cocaine."

"I don't get it."

Hamson sat up and stared Buzz directly in the face. "I feel personally involved in this operation, Colonel. I really do. I had a best pal at the academy, a guy named Vinnie DiSabato. He was from New York City, a big hard robust Italian, who was using the academy to get out from under the life his family had led in one of the worse sections of Manhattan.

"I was pulling for that guy, more than anyone else. We were...we were like brothers. You know how it can be in the academy."

"Yeah, sure I do," Buzz answered his junior officer. He did remember the way those powerful relationships between fellow cadets were bonded in the pressure-cooker atmosphere of the military academy.

"Well, DiSabato was a hell-raiser, a great guy at a party. He would pull his weight in anything, but he also was the one who would lead the way when it came to blowing off steam. There were stories.... I didn't believe them, but there were stories....

"Time went on, things were getting close to graduation, and DiSabato started to weird out on me, his best buddy, his pal. He wouldn't show up for appointments, he wouldn't be there for a study session, things like that. I didn't want to see what was happening, so I ignored it as long as I could. Maybe I could have done something if I'd . . .''

Buzz felt a tug of empathy for the pain he saw on the younger man's face. But he knew it would be best to let Hamson work it through on his own. He sat silently and waited for the lieutenant to continue.

"It was coke, the fast-lane cocaine that was exactly what DiSabato was trying to get away from. It caught him at the Point. Maybe it just never let go. Maybe it was always there, but he'd controlled it for the first couple years. I don't know. I never will. Vinnie had become . . .'' Mike turned away from Buzz as though he couldn't handle relating the story to the older man while looking at him.

"He'd been stealing from Company funds to pay for his habit, and from other cadets, but that's not how they caught him. It was a routine physical where the medics discovered that he'd damned near ruined his nasal membranes with the stuff. A urinalysis confirmed their suspicion. There was only one explanation, and that meant he was out on his ass.

"DiSabato went back to the city without talking to me, and I never heard from him again. I tried—over and over again—to reach him, but it didn't work. It was too late. I guess he was too embarrassed.

"I heard he was destroyed by it all, and especially by the fact that he had caused it himself. He felt he had no one else to blame. So he took it out on the one target he had. He ended up jumping off a skyscraper, falling from so high that he was demolished when he hit the ground. They could barely find enough pieces of him to make an identification."

Now Mike did look to Buzz, and the colonel could see a tear streaming down each of the lieutenant's cheeks. He wasn't a man who would make a scene, but he wasn't afraid to admit his pain at a friend's death.

"I don't think I could have made it through my plebe year if it hadn't been for that guy, Colonel. I *knew* him. I knew him inside and out. There was no way he was going to do something as stupid as ruining his career and his life over cocaine if it was just a party drug. It was something more than that. It was a poison that got into a good man and it killed him.

"Colonel, I *want* this assignment. I want it because I want to end it, this drug traffic that gets into every single part of American life and destroys people and their dreams and their families."

Buzz looked at Mike and nodded his head slowly. He understood his lieutenant even better now, and he was even happier that Hamson was going along with him to Bolivia on their mission as "advisers" to the Bolivian National Guard.

THE HUEY HELICOPTER'S distinctive *whoop, whoop, whoop* sounded as the chopper skimmed along the treetops of the Chapare.

Buzz McDonough looked down at the incredibly lush growth underneath the Huey. He hadn't thought it would ever happen, but the words of the agricultural lecturer came back to him. No wonder all those people had misjudged the potential of the soil. There wasn't a single spot for miles around, even at that low altitude, where anyone could see the ground. The trees of the Chapare covered everything from view.

The many tall variations of mahogany and palm looked as though they must be springing up from the richest soil in the world. But, if that academic was right, the earth they were rooted in was actually so thin and weak that even a single wheat crop would exhaust it. Once those trees with their widespread narrow roots were gone, the first tropical rain storm would send most of the topsoil rushing down to the tributaries, then on to the Amazon to be swept into the Atlantic, never to be regained for cultivation.

The noise of the rotors was intense enough to make conversation difficult, and Buzz had to yell into Mike Hamson's ear to be heard. "Your men ready?"

Mike gave Buzz a thumbs-up sign and big grin. He was ready for the mission, and he'd thrown his all into preparing the two dozen troops for their tasks.

The force was top-heavy with officers. Such a small task force didn't really call for both colonel and two lieutenants, but the diplomatic and political sensitivities of the action had dictated an officer of McDonough's seniority, and it was determined that the "loots" were necessary because the mission was also considered a training exercise for the Bolivian National Guardsmen.

It had been quickly established, though, that the Bolivians wouldn't have responded to anyone but Jesus Christ himself, and even that seemed questionable to McDonough after the time and energy he'd seen Mike and Swanson, the other lieutenant, put into the preparation for Operation Manufacture. Buzz had complained vehemently when he discovered he wasn't going to get any of the Leopards, the vicious but effective Bolivian antidrug forces who'd been used in previous joint operations.

The Bolivians they did get were all Indian, some kind of Inca descendants, Buzz figured. They were full of somewhat overblown native pride and seemed to practice a native religion with great fervor while they claimed to be Roman Catholic with equal verve. None of the Americans understood the language, though they all had been needlessly chosen for their Spanish-language skills. Once they'd left the capital city of La Paz, it had become apparent that Spanish was the narrow preserve of the upper classes.

The officers and the noncoms and enlisted men who were part of the American contingent had done everything they could to put the group together and to try to establish an esprit de corps with the National Guardsmen, but to no avail.

Theirs was strictly a split-personality force. The Americans would provide their skills in their areas, and the National Guardsmen would go on their own. The only possible lines of communication between the two groups were between the highest officers. Even there, the Spanish language wasn't necessary, since the two Bolivians in charge of the native force spoke flawless English, which they had learned, McDonough discovered, at the University of Miami.

Roderiguiz was the name of the Bolivian in charge. McDonough moved over to squat next to him and check on last-minute details as the American-piloted Hueys approached their destination. "All set, Miguel?"

"You got it, Colonel," the other man said. He couldn't have been any older than Hamson, and he was certainly much less well trained. Buzz had discovered that Roderiguiz had been in ROTC at Miami and then had moved directly to the officers corps of the Bolivian National Guard thanks to a rich father who was the heir to a tin-mining fortune.

"Okay, your men have to take the lead with the small firearms," Buzz said, repeating the plan, though he knew that even a dimwit like Roderiguiz must have these simple strategies memorized. "You have to deal with the armed guards. Our men will handle the demolition of the factory."

"Right," Roderiguiz said. McDonough could read the man's contempt on his face. Roderiguiz was puffing on a huge, smelly cigar, using it as a little token of his contempt for the American colonel. McDonough wasn't going to rise to such small-time bait. He moved away from the unprofessional odor and smoke of the stogie and went back to sit by Hamson. Buzz could only hope that the natives wouldn't screw anything up.

The sounds of the Huey's rotors seemed to slow, a clear signal they were approaching their destination.

The cocaine factory had been identified and located by officers from the Drug Enforcement Administration. The American DEA had turned itself into a major international intelligence operation in recent years. In order to fight the flood of illicit drugs that was moving across United States borders, it had moved into fields once the exclusive domain of the CIA and its military counterparts.

This time, Buzz hoped, there would be a factory. On previous attempts by the American military to move inside the borders of Bolivia, the plans had been leaked ahead of time, giving the drug smugglers ample opportunity to pack up their stuff and melt into the jungle.

The anger of the American Congress had been enough to scare the Bolivians into pledges of greater secrecy and cooperation than they had shown before. The promise of payments to the peasants had played major role in getting past the objections of the fake politicians in the Bolivian capital. McDonough and most of the rest of the American military and drug enforcement establishment were convinced La Paz was the single most corrupt city in the world.

The Huey began to descend more quickly. Buzz leaned out the wide door of the chopper and signaled his men to get ready. There, just beneath them, was the first clearing he'd seen in many miles. There was a thick trail of smoke rising from a long tin-roofed building on the edge of the opening. That was the factory!

Buzz felt a surge of excitement. He had just seen the concrete sign hinting at the possibility that the whole thing would go well, after all.

The rotors of the helicopters were still moving fast enough after it had hit the ground that they created a stormlike wind, sending debris rushing through the air, scattering the remains of cooking fires and overturning utensils.

The American soldiers and Bolivian National Guardsmen efficiently got out of their carriers and stood in loose formation on the ground. Then the Bolivians followed Roderiguiz's barked orders and moved quickly to encircle the small factory, each one holding a U.S. issue M-16.

Buzz stood and watched the entire maneuver with growing discomfort. There was too little to the whole thing, he thought as he walked up to the entrance of the factory and looked in. He could identify the setup as a traditional hydrochloride distillation lab. The arrangements of tubes and glass beakers had a makeshift look, as though the place had been built by high school students for a science project.

His eyes scanned the rest of the area. That was what was troubling him about all of this. There were dozens of locals, all of them wearing their distinctive rimmed hats, the unique part of the costume of the Andes tribes. They were scowling at him, hating him and the rest of the Americans. He followed the line of their vision and realized, too, that they hated the Bolivian National Guard officers just as much—but not the local troops themselves. For the enlisted men the locals sent out secret smiles and knowing glances.

That was the moment when Colonel McDonough knew they'd been had. "Hamson!" he called out. The lieutenant ran over to him and took only a single second to take in the way the colonel had lifted up his M-16 into a position ready for firing. "Something's way off, Lieutenant. I want the men on those choppers now."

"But, sir, the factory—"

"That was a direct order, Lieutenant. I said *now*."

McDonough's actions hadn't gone unnoticed by the Bolivian National Guardsmen. Without a word from their officers, they lifted their own M-16s. Buzz dropped to the ground, damning his thirty-eight years and the muscles that weren't as supple as they used to be and were letting him know that as they objected to the quick, rough treatment he was giving them.

"Get down, Mike!" Buzz screamed.

But it was too late. Hamson had already turned to relay the colonel's original order. He was the first to be hit by the fusillade of hot metal that the Bolivians' M-16s sent flying through the air. The bullets pounded into his exposed back, making his body jump with the force of each round that slammed against it.

The Americans had been sent here to work with the National Guardsmen. The soldiers had been told that their supposed enemy were drug manufacturers and smugglers, and they weren't on the defensive against the uniformed Bolivian troops. The automatic rifle fire kept up a deadly serenade as it swept through the Americans, who were conveniently clustered together, leaving most of them dead before they could know what was happening.

Buzz McDonough had cut his teeth in Vietnam. He'd been in Grenada and he'd seen time as an "adviser" in Honduras. He knew what battle was, and he knew when it wasn't going to go his way.

He desperately looked over to the nearest Huey and saw that the pilot was slumped over his controls. The lethal wound hadn't been from rifles; Buzz could see the grim evidence of a knife in a bloody cut baring the insides of the man's neck. The guardsmen had taken care of the fly-boys first.

Buzz began to answer the National Guard fire. The native troops weren't used to a good fight from anyone, and they retreated at the initial response to their surprise attack. Buzz took a couple of them out as they tried to reach the wall of jungle surrounding the clearing.

The reactions of a man in battle were swimming through Buzz's head. Survival was the first and foremost of them. He had to get out, and his whole being was directed toward escaping the ambush.

Sorrow was another, but he had to demand that his mind forget the sight of young Hamson being cut down so ruthlessly.

Fear was still another, the one that was always with a man in a firefight. The loud noises of dozens of M-16s shooting off seemed to fuel the adrenaline pouring through his veins. His nervous system was on overload as it tried to sort out all the sensations bombarding him with the relentlessness of the fire that was digging up small pieces of Amazon dirt all around him.

The Bolivians had been lucky to get the Americans by surprise. Only the sheer quantity of their fire and the proximity of their targets had allowed them to get so many of the highly skilled troops. When they had to aim and fire from a greater distance, they were proving to be poor marksmen.

McDonough wasn't going to test their ability that much, but he felt he had a chance to get to the laboratory building and make use of its cover. The structure was only a short distance away, maybe a few dozen feet from his naked position in the clearing.

Buzz stood up and began to make a run for it. A stream of bullets created a dancing line of eruptions in the ground behind him. Then the projectiles began to change their tune, into a chorus of pings as the automatic fire hit harmlessly on the metal sides of the building.

"Roderiguiz!" Buzz turned his M-16 to the Bolivian officer huddling inside and was ready to pull the trigger to avenge himself on at least that one son of a bitch. The look of utter panic on Miguel's face saved his life—for a minute, at least.

"What the hell is going on?" McDonough demanded.

"The damned idiots!" Roderiguiz exclaimed. "I didn't know—you have to believe me."

"What? Tell me, asshole, before I blow you away!"

"The guardsmen they sent with us, they're all from this region. I had no way of knowing that until we got here and I could see and hear them talking with the others. They could speak the local dialect, all of them. Someone in La Paz set both of us up."

A fresh round of fire exploded many of the beakers and made the two men hug the ground more for cover.

Buzz unloosed a round from his own M-16 out into the jungle, trying to teach someone there a lesson. "But what the hell . . ."

"Don't you see? These are the sons of the peasants here. We're taking away their parents' livelihood. They're stopping us from turning their families into paupers."

"The American money . . ." Buzz began to say.

But there was no answer. Just then, a new line of fire opened up behind them. Buzz turned to face it as he slammed a new clip in his rifle, but instead he froze as he watched the new bullets perform their ritual. They were dancing up the side of the building, directly toward a couple of dozen five-gallon containers. Each one was marked Explosives.

McDonough froze. He watched the wildly flying bullets from the Bolivians as they playfully approached and moved away from the danger. He could read the labels clearly: the drums contained ether. One of the required ingredients in the cocaine distillation process, ether, Buzz knew, was highly volatile. Its eruption in deadly explosions was the cause of the death of many a criminal in back-alley cocaine operations.

Suddenly the bullets began another movement, and one of them hit the bottom of the stack of ether.

Buzz felt a sudden flash of red heat. And then he felt nothing, ever again.

THE GUARDSMEN WATCHED the enormous explosion with glee, until they realized that the burning debris from the fire show was beginning to rain down on them. They ran back into the forest for cover. The damp, wet jungle didn't feed the embers. In only a short while, they emerged into the clearing again and looked at the smoldering mess that had once been the factory.

The entire thing was a total loss. Shrugging unconcernedly, not for one instant caring about the American dead or the Bolivian officers, for that matter, they stripped out of their uniforms and changed into the civilian clothing of the Chapare peasant that their families had brought for them. Moving among the corpses, they scavenged some mementos as well as items to sell in the marketplace: handguns, medals, fancy wristwatches and wallets with valuable American dollars disappeared into their pockets.

It had all gone as planned by their real leaders, the local soldiers told one another. Their families' livelihood was secure, and they could go back to the lives they had always led before.

They would disappear into the facelessness of the peasant of the Chapare, and their brief interval as members of the Bolivian National Guard would never be mentioned again.

The people in La Paz were very powerful. They would make sure that the event was all forgotten.

3

Walker Jessup quivered with anticipation. The whole of his large, rotund body seemed to be shaking as he sat at the small table at the New Orleans Emporium in the Adams-Morgan section of Washington, D.C.

He'd had to travel far from his regular haunts in Georgetown and Capitol Hill, the district neighborhoods where Jessup usually dined. But he knew it was going to be worth having come all the way out to the newly chic Adams-Morgan just for the sake of the meal he was about to start.

The first piece of evidence was already in front of him. Jessup reached over to pick up one of the small shrimp that were the special appetizers of the authentically Cajun eatery. He ignored the rest of the diners around him, too taken with his own immense pleasure to care about other human beings.

The shrimp slipped into his mouth, and he bit down on it, elated by an explosion of flavorful delight in his taste buds.

Jessup closed his eyes with sheer exuberant joy. There was nothing—certainly not even sex—that could make a man like him feel so alive, so complete, so happy as a fine meal such as the one the New Orleans Emporium was delivering to him. The plate of appetizers was only the foreplay of his evening. The real thing was yet to come.

Jessup had to fight his base desire to finish off the appetizers too quickly. He wanted to savor each one of the small crustaceans in its Cajun piquant sauce and only sip the white Chablis he'd ordered to go with them. But there was a drive inside him urging him to go on, faster. The drive was propelled by the fear that the conscientious and friendly waiting staff might think that the presence of the shrimp on Jessup's plate meant that he wanted them to hesitate before beginning the main course.

The main course!

The mere thought of it sent a tremor through Jessup's bulk and brought his eyelids together in a sweetly painful motion of wonder. He'd heard so much about it, he'd waited so long for it, he'd dreamed of it for so many nights! No man had ever looked forward to a rendezvous with the woman of his dreams with more intensity or less patience than Walker Jessup had contemplated his meeting with the New Orleans Emporium's pan-blackened prime rib of beef.

A small whimper flew from his throat as the actual name of this delight crossed his mind. Saliva marshaled its forces in his mouth, and he had to use his tongue to fight back its flood in a deep, masculine swallow.

"Are you done with the first course, sir?" the waitress asked.

Jessup looked up to her and could only nod. Once she took away that plate of shrimp, he thought, he'd be that much closer to *it*. He watched the friendly young woman depart from the table and wondered if the chef was a sadist. If he was, then it might be hours yet before... But, no! There, already, the waitress was returning. On her arm was a platter, and she seemed to be coming toward him.

Jessup's eyes closed once more. He tried to will them open to watch the approach of the prime rib, but then the sharp smell of its spices swept into his consciousness like a body blow.

"Will there be anything else, sir?" the waitress asked politely.

"No, no..." Now Jessup was able to force his eyelids apart to look down at...perfection! The sight in front of him was one of the most beautiful pieces of art he'd ever seen in his life. The perfect slice of highest quality beef was spread over the white porcelain, whose light color only intensified the impression of the blackened surface of the prime rib.

Jessup picked up his knife and fork and held them over the prime rib, his saliva running like a springtime flood, his mouth quivering with delight at what was going to come.

He put the fork's tines through the beef and knew from the way they simply melted into the flesh that the prime rib was more than simply tender. It was the perfection of the bull. He moved his knife down slowly to place the edge at the top of the tenderloin. Letting it slide through the beef with slow and deliberate movements, he cut the first morsel. It was ready for him and him alone, like the virgin of his dreams.

Jessup lifted the fork up to his lips, opened them so wide that a couple at the next table gasped at the obscenity and then...

A shadow fell over Jessup's table. He looked at its outline and froze in dread. The fork that had so recently been ready to deliver its cargo slowly descended, and the beef stuck on its tines seemed to begin to lose its grace and to go flaccid when it hit the plate.

"He wants to see you, right away."

Jessup had known who it was even before he heard that voice, but the voice of the efficient Miss Roseline confirmed her loathsome identity.

The whimper coming from Jessup was that of a sorrowful puppy. "Can't it wait? Just for a while?" He hated the sound of his own weakness as he begged her for a moment's reprieve. He was still staring at the prime rib coated with the superb and incomparable preparations of the New Orleans Emporium. "Please!"

"The car's waiting outside. It's parked illegally. I don't want the driver to have any problems. It is imperative that you come with me now."

The words were clipped in that not quite human voice of hers. There was no compassion in her body. There was no compassion in her soul—if she had one!

Jessup was suddenly swept up in a tidal wave of rage. "Who cares about the goddamned driver! You're interfering with my dinner!"

If she caught the deep and powerful meaning that Jessup conveyed when he uttered the religious words—dinner— Miss Roseline ignored it.

"Please, Mr. Jessup, you know we wouldn't approach you unless it were utterly necessary. There's a situation demanding your immediate attention. I've already settled your bill. Shall we?"

Her question was pure rhetoric and they both knew it. She swiveled on her high heels and made for the door. The very idea that she'd paid for the meal meant that his abandonment of it was all the more painful. To think he could have eaten that dinner and not have to put down the hard cash for it! It was too much to bear to think that the two passions of Walker Jessup's life—gluttony and greed—would have been merged in that one slab of perfectly prepared pan-blackened prime rib!

He had no choice. He stood and put his napkin over the lonely beef, as a mourner would cover a loved one with a shroud, and he followed her outside.

The senator's stretch Cadillac limousine was waiting at the door. The chauffeur held the door open for Jessup's huge body. Walker fell into the car and back against the plush seat just as the door slammed.

Walker Jessup knew that most men in the world would have been delighted to be alone under these circumstances with Miss Roseline. She was, in addition to being an unbelievably effective and efficient secretary, quite beautiful. Her skin was clear, and her light makeup highlighted the beauty of her eyes. Her body was chicly encased in a suit of the latest fashion. Other men could never have thought of food at such a moment, so close to a woman as desirable as she. But Jessup simply couldn't forget the partner he'd left at the table inside the restaurant.

"I'm sure cook can come up with something for you," Miss Roseline said in a strained attempt at friendly conversation. "Perhaps a sandwich."

Walker Jessup understood the meaning of the cliché; his blood boiled. His entire body seemed to be grabbed by hot fury. At least, he realized, he was forgetting his dinner. Instead he was now contemplating homicide.

"WALKER, MY FRIEND! Come in, have a seat. A drink perhaps? A bourbon for Mr. Jessup, Miss Roseline."

Whenever the senator was in a particular kind of friendly good humor, Jessup knew there was real trouble involved. He slyly studied the older man and wondered what was happening. The *Washington Post* had been reporting increased terrorist activities coming out of Iran. The *New York Times* was giving front-page play to North Korea's threats regarding its border with South Korea. The *Boston Globe* was convinced that there had been a new covert initiative against the Nicaraguan regime. Any one of those were possibilities. But that was unlikely. Things already in the newspapers were seldom the projects into which the senator called Jessup.

The secretary delivered Jessup's drink. He sipped the bourbon and knew it was Wild Turkey, smooth and aged for many years. A slight bit of his antagonism toward the woman melted away. She could have given him the senator's more common pour, a sufficient bourbon, but not Wild Turkey. He was willing to take the premium liquor as a gesture on her part and, while he wasn't about to smile at her in appreciation, a little of the glower did evaporate.

"We seem to have a slight problem, Walker." The senator smiled that smile of his that he thought made him seem charming. The actual effect was grotesque. The beady eyes that betrayed the senator's shifty political personality couldn't ever be compensated for by a simple smile. When the senator did affect this look, it intensified the onlooker's conviction that he was truly evil.

Not in the devilish sense. No, the senator was evil in the simple American political sense. Years ago, there must have been some ideal that had propelled a young man into the political arena. He must have had some higher aspirations lead him into the battles between ideological forces. Whatever those were, they'd been washed out of him by decades on the Hill. Now he only understood power and the importance of its use.

Jessup had heard the senator speak in favor of lowering the minimum wage in one state and then, on the same day, demand it be raised in the neighboring one. The audience got whatever it wanted to hear from the senator, and so did every official and journalist in Washington.

Now, after an accident that had unfortunately involved some of Jessup's own compatriots, the senator was doing his speaking from a wheelchair. What would have been a psychological disaster for most men actually proved a blessing for the senator. Washington gossip said that his sex life had been brought to an end by the accident that had forced him into the chair. If so, it had also ended the one part of his life capable of bringing him down in scandal, especially during the current ultrarighteous chapter of American political history, when no presidential candidate dared appear on a public forum without his wife.

There was another, unexpected bonus to the wheelchair. As the senator had grown old, his worst features came to the fore, as though the callus principles and withered ethics of his life needed to rise to the surface of his skin and rest there, demanding to be in public view. Whatever softness or even sincerity had been a part of the senator's visage before had been erased by the hard fights and back-alley tactics of federal politics.

The wheelchair actually gave the man a semblance of humanity. Old ladies crooned over him. Young women felt pity. Men felt empathy. The wheelchair had taken a barbarian and given him an infirmity that helped protect him from his foes. Who could say bad things about an old man confined to a wheelchair?

Well, actually, Jessup could have. He could have said plenty. More than anyone else, Jessup knew the secrets of the senator and his cronies in Washington. They had need for means to ensure that American policies were carried out even when they were illegal. Unlike some people who had been involved in recent scandals in the White House, the senator and his pals knew enough not to involve the actual government in their schemes.

Instead, they turned to Jessup. A former CIA power, Jessup had earned the name "the Fixer" through his many activities. He was the one who could make things right in the world when they seemed to be going wrong and when the powers that be at the Pentagon or at the CIA's headquarters in Langley weren't up to the job, or found themselves held back by laws.

The senator just then took his own drink from Miss Roseline and made a fake-friendly toast toward Walker. The secretary withdrew to stand by the far wall, close enough to hear everything going on, but not so close that she intruded on the conversation. Jessup was too smart to forget her. He was also smart enough to realize that her presence was irrelevant; the senator would tell her everything that was said, in any event.

"Well, Senator, what seems to be so very pressing that a man has to be taken away from his supper?"

Jessup's memory of that once-loved roast beef was actually fading as he sat there in the senator's study. He knew that he would have to have all his faculties focused on what was said next. Even something as rare and honored as the memory of his dinner had to be sacrificed for his duty. Jessup was only playing with the other man by bringing up the inconvenience of the unscheduled meeting.

"Minor issues, really quite minor, indeed. There does seem to be something of great interest to us that we would like to have taken care of. I'm sure that your . . . friends will be quite able to do the job quickly and quietly."

The smile that broadened unwillingly across the senator's face told Jessup that it was going to be a really good one. If the old man had to protest so very much, then there was a lot of trouble somewhere.

"What might those 'minor issues' be and, just as important, where?"

The senator scowled, an expression much more characteristic of his true nature than the former attempted smile had been. "Drugs. Bolivia."

Jessup knew that the senator's quick surrender meant that something very major was up. If it had been otherwise, the man would have played more cat-and-mouse games with him. "Well, that's not new. After all, Bolivia's been the source of most of the cocaine that's been imported into the United States for decades, and you have your various programs in place. What would you ever need my people for?''

"Sweden's involved, as well.'' Now the senator *really* scowled. A dark cloud seemed to form on his forehead, in the midst of his ancient wrinkles. "High technology. International intrigue. Endangered governments. Bah!'' The senator knocked back the whole of his drink and held the empty glass toward Miss Roseline, silently demanding a refill.

"Do tell, Senator.'' It was Jessup's turn to put on a false smile now. "Do tell all about it.''

The senator waited for his new drink. Once it had been put in his hand by the ever-present Miss Roseline, he began. "Our troops down there have been having trouble with the Bolivians. It hasn't been in the papers....''

"Operation Manufacture.'' Jessup had spoken the words like a poker player slamming down a wild card on the table in front of an unsuspecting foe. The senator was obviously stunned that Jessup knew about the top-secret operation. "It's my business to know about these things,'' Jessup said by way of an explanation.

"Not when they happen to *us*, it isn't,'' the senator retorted. It took him a moment and a large sip of bourbon to regain his composure. "It appears that the new president, Alfonso Martinez, who just took power in La Paz a few months ago, doesn't have control of all of the military. Some factions have never had any intention of giving support to the undertaking.

"But the failure has backfired on them. There are many powerful forces in the house and the senate who are up in arms about the whole thing. They threatened to cut off all of our military aid to Bolivia and to ban its legal imports into this country besides, something that will backfire on us if it means we end up destabilizing Martinez's fragile regime even more.

"One of the generals—Valdez—is as slimy as they come. We're on the lookout for him, in particular. All our intelligence points to a probable coup by him, and soon. I'm afraid Martinez isn't worth saving. Those South American countries just don't nurture good government.

"Of course, that's not always bad, since sometimes it works to our advantage when the dictators are anti-Communist." The senator's first truly warm smile of the evening showed just how emphatically he believed that statement. "That man Valdez wants the whole thing: he doesn't like sharing his power, even with fellow army officers.

"Well, he's certainly not going to go out on a limb for Martinez, I can tell you that. There's nothing a corrupt military like Bolivia's hates more than an interfering civilian like Martinez.

"We'd always assumed that Valdez was in on the drug smuggling. His social companions aren't exactly on the hit parade at the Drug Enforcement Administration. In fact, the DEA has him on a secret list of drug exporters, personally. But there's a problem...."

The senator's voice trailed off, and a new expression crossed his face. Jessup understood that the old man was actually very puzzled by something. "It seems," the senator finally continued, "that since the fiasco with Operation Manufacture, Valdez is actually moving against the cocaine dealers. His own troops are closing down the distilleries in the Chapare, and he finally started on the relocation of the natives to new land in the El Beni department of Bolivia, land where they can actually be expected to grow edible crops."

"Then why do you need me?" Jessup asked.

"Because, while all of that is happening, the flow of cocaine out of Bolivia has not decreased. They might be relying on stockpiles now, but someone is working to erase the possibility that those stores could be replaced. We, ourselves, had finally owned up to the idea that the Bolivian economy would collapse without some support, at least for the duration of a transition out of drugs into other forms of income production, if we simply eradicated coca cultivation. President Martinez just couldn't have been expected to keep the government running and the country under his control if he continued with his program.

"In the meantime, though, especially after the furor from the death of the American soldiers in Operation Manufacture—"

"A helicopter crash, if I recall the news reports," Jessup interjected, knowing perfectly well what had actually happened. He also understood that the Washington establishment had had to come up with and stick by that story. The public uproar over those deaths had been difficult enough to handle when everyone thought the cause was accidental. If it had ever leaked out that the American troops had been slaughtered by La Paz's own National Guardsmen, then there would have been hell to pay.

The senator didn't rise to the bait, but went on. "The cocaine is still coming into the United States. It is still originating in Bolivia. It is no longer being grown as extensively as it was. Therefore, there is a major cache of the drug in that country.

"We want it destroyed.

"And we want to make sure that there's nothing going on to secretly replenish it. We're making major inroads now on the Chapare's production of the drug. We don't want any surprises after these successes."

"You mentioned Sweden," Jessup interrupted rudely and with little regret for it. "What could the Swedes possibly have to do with all of this?"

Miss Roseline, the source of more secret information in Washington than the FBI, spoke emotionlessly from her perch in the corner. "The Swedish prime minister who was recently assassinated in Stockholm studied chemistry as an undergraduate. It appears, from what our sources report, that he was very, very upset about something he'd stumbled onto in the archives of the Gustavus Adolphus Institute.

"We haven't any idea what that was. The institute is a research institution, and its whole philosophy is to encourage experimentation by its staff.

"The prime minister used to make a nuisance of himself by roaming through the institute and personally monitoring the staff's activities."

"You think that's why he was killed? The chief of state of a neutral country found something in those files that would lead to murder?"

Miss Roseline clearly found Jessup's question needless rhetoric. "The prime minister had been talking obliquely to a few colleagues about a scientific horror. They'd assumed he'd discovered nuclear experimentation that, while outlawed in Sweden, is clearly within their technological grasp.

"But the day after the assassination, one of the leading chemists at Gustavus Adolphus disappeared. No one really put it all together—we don't think the Swedes have, themselves—but there were large amounts of cocaine found in the scientist's laboratory.

"Closer examination showed that the molecular structure was...off."

"So, the guy had some bum blow, big deal." Walker squirmed in his seat. The senator was taking his time getting to the point, and Jessup was beginning to feel he was submitted to undue stress with his dinner being delayed.

"Mr. Jessup, we think the difference in the makeup of the drug indicates that it was synthesized," Miss Roseline summed up curtly.

"The goddamn bastard has made artificial cocaine," the senator muttered. "Can you imagine what that could mean? If there's a way to put cheap, easily manufactured drugs on the streets of America..."

The image was suddenly clear in Jessup's mind, and he eyed the senator shrewdly while he spoke. "So, you think the Bolivians have him. That he's set himself up with a new kind of factory in South America. The Bolivians are playing along with your games and eradicating their natural supply of coca because they don't need it anymore. They have a new source."

"Find it, Jessup," the senator commanded. "Find the cache of cocaine they're using now and find that damn factory and blow it and everyone concerned with it to hell."

"Senator, the drug dealers in places like Bolivia and Colombia are better equipped and better trained than any of the formal armed forces on the rest of the South American continent. I don't know if my people can actually take on that big an assignment."

Jessup's ploy was just a part of their usual game. Of course the SOBs would take the assignment—they always did. But there was also always a little maneuvering between the Fixer and the senator over the pay the men should receive. But it seemed at the present that the senator was bent on depriving Jessup his enjoyment.

"For a half million dollars apiece, I'm sure they'll see the way," the senator spit out. Then, to announce Jessup's dismissal, he turned on the electric motor powering his chair. "See to the details, Miss Roseline. I'm off to bed."

The chair whirred into another room, and the senator disappeared.

"Well, Mr. Jessup, would you like to have that sandwich now, or shall we get down to basics?"

Jessup felt a growl building in his stomach. "Let's do both at the same time, shall we?"

What a life he led.

4

Liam O'Toole jumped through the burning wreckage of the crashed helicopter with an M-16 in each hand. He lifted the two rifles over his head and began to shoot automatic rounds into the air. The lethal rifles leveled downward, and their torrent of lead flew through the air, cutting through the chests of the one hundred Vietnamese who were standing in front of him, their own AK-47s silent or else firing uselessly into the air around Liam, each one missing him by a mile. Small explosions of blood and shredded flesh sailed like missiles through the sky, dropping disgusting evidence of the carnage O'Toole was causing all around the smoldering fuselage of the downed helicopter.

When the few remaining Vietnamese understood how hopeless their cause was, they threw their weapons to the earth and prostrated themselves in front of the godlike American, begging for salvation and life.

O'Toole's chiseled face—a perfect match to his sculpted bare-chested torso—had a look of contempt for his conquered foes. It was obvious that only massive self-discipline kept him from delivering coups de grace to the unworthy enemies.

But O'Toole wasn't a man to give in to a base lack of self-discipline. He clenched his teeth—a motion that produced a tightening of his facial muscles and his neck tendons—and kept himself under control. The victory was his as it was. He didn't need to prove any more to these gooks.

O'Toole's flawless muscles glistened with sweat and grime as his massive pectorals jumped in the bright light that emphasized their manly strength.

Liam moved through the Vietnamese as the survivors moved apart and away from him, much as the Red Sea accommodated Moses, and he looked around at the small mound of dead corpses his M-16s had just created. He dropped to his knees and lifted his head to display a tragic defiance and pride in the line of his jaw.

"This is for America!" the warrior proclaimed.

The only problem was, he wasn't Liam O'Toole. The real Liam O'Toole was watching the whole scene in utter horror.

"Cut!" the director screamed offstage.

Mercifully, the actors stood up, exposing the apparently dead Vietnamese as shams. They were refugees and the children of refugees from the Communist regime, imported from the Little Saigon neighborhood of Los Angeles to play the roles of their own enemies.

"What a crock of shit," one of the men said out loud as he looked at the red dye covering his body strategically, its timing and location carefully produced by the special effects staff, most of whom were now rushing through the crew to inspect their handiwork.

"I'll say," another Vietnamese-American declared as he pushed and shoved his way out from under a pile of his former high school playmates. "I don't think that's the way it happened, asshole."

He was speaking to Malcolm MacMalcolm, the onetime megastar of Hollywood whose advancing years had finally forced him to resign his position as the leading man of the cinema and to instead assume the role of producer/director of his own movies.

MacMalcolm ignored the complaints of the extras and moved toward his protégé, Nick Falucci. Once a gold medalist on the U.S. Olympic water polo team, Falucci's most recent claim to fame had been posing in a centerfold for *Playgirl* magazine. It had inspired so much confidence in the aspiring young star that half of Hollywood had rushed to sign him to a contract.

"Nick! Nick! You were superb. In that one scene was every young American's desire to win!"

"Did my makeup smear?" the athlete asked with great concern. "I really hope it looked all right. And you got my left side, didn't you? It's my best side, Malcolm."

"Do you mean your left ball or your right ball's your best side?" Liam O'Toole asked, his voice straining.

"Oh," Nick Falucci said with all sincerity, "I don't do frontal nudity. I mean on my cheek. The cheek on my face." Just to make sure that Liam knew what he meant, the actor pointed to himself.

It was too much for Liam. He pulled back his fist and saw the perfect target that the twerp was actually showing to him.

"No! Liam, please, you simply have got to control yourself." Malcolm MacMalcolm then turned toward Nick and patted him on the arm. "You were just fine, just fine. Why don't you go on now. We're done for the day."

Nick threw a disdainful look at the real O'Toole and turned on his heels to withdraw.

"Why do you continue to be so difficult with the boy?" Malcolm demanded when he and Liam were alone.

"He's supposed to be me!" Liam complained. "He's supposed to be making a movie based on my poems. This piece of shit hasn't anything to do with my writing, with my life, with my experience, with *anyone's* experiences in Vietnam.

"Malcolm, you can't fire off two M-16s at the same time and, even if you could, only a fool would waste his ammunition by firing it into the air. And that last line: 'This is for America!' Where did you get that crap! I'm as patriotic as any man, but I never..."

"Liam, you must understand that this is Hollywood." He struggled with his concentration, trying to come up with something that would make his vision of moviemaking intelligible to the hulking Irishman. "You know all about poetic license, and well, this is cinematic license. We have to take the whole of your literary works, and we have got to be able to—"

"Don't give me this," Liam growled as he turned and began to walk off the set, actually forcing the crew to make way for him and his obvious anger much more authentically than his theatrical double had done earlier. O'Toole had at least as many muscles, and they were at least as big as the actor's. The major difference between the two men's bodies was that the real Liam's skin wasn't unflawed: it had been cut and stitched from countless battle wounds, leaving a patchwork of scars over him. That realism was something the men at work weren't going to test.

Malcolm MacMalcolm wasn't about to let any of his profits walk out in such a manner. He had visions of a publicity tour so the veteran mercenary could promote his movie—and MacMalcolm's investment. He'd seen visions of the handsome soldier-for-hire on talk shows from Des Moines to Cleveland and from Seattle to Miami. The movie was a loser and didn't have a chance without a marketing ploy like that. MacMalcolm had been around Tinseltown long enough to smell a skunk. And this one stank! he conceded wryly to himself.

"Liam—" He'd caught up with the Irishman on the edge of the set and grabbed hold of his biceps. "Now, calm down. Think of the *money*! You've already made a fortune from this film, and there's more. You have a percentage—"

"The only percentage I care about right now," O'Toole broke in, "is the very small percentage of my dignity that I have left. You've ruined my words. There's not a single line of my poetry left in that script after the way the five teams of hack writers you hired have mauled it. And that mannequin made a big mistake when he put his clothes back on. Maybe some teenage girls don't mind looking at his butt, but it's the only part of him with any talent. Cover it up, and you have nothing."

"But, Liam, I tell you, once this movie is made, your poetry is going to sell like a Judith Krantz novel. They're all going to line up for it in stores...."

"Malcolm, that's another thing. You told me the poems would be published. That was part of the deal. Where's the contract for that, huh? You've taken me, Malcolm. I'm not standing around to be made a fool of anymore."

Liam wrenched his arm from the other man's grip and stormed away. He didn't hear the cheers of the Vietnamese extras who'd overheard the whole thing. He didn't care.

The one thing in life Liam O'Toole had always wanted was to be a poet. He'd gotten through the civil wars of a dozen countries and the campaigns of a dozen armies. He'd suffered untold amounts of rejection and dismissal at the hands of crude agents, unfeeling editors and profit-driven publishers. He'd spent every spare moment he could working on his writing, attending workshops, studying in adult education courses.

It had never worked. That is, at one time he had managed to get fifty volumes printed through a vanity press, but when marketing efforts had failed him, he had "bequeathed" the books to a disinterested bystander.

Then, when he had last been with the SOBs on an assignment in the South Pacific, he'd met up with Malcolm MacMalcolm, the star of stars, the hero of as many movies as O'Toole had been of real battles. The actor had promised him fame and fortune—neither of which Liam really cared about—but he had also promised Liam that the same fame and fortune would mean his book would be in print.

He would be a published author.

Even as Liam tore through the lot of Celestial Studios in the San Fernando Valley—where movies were really made, not in Hollywood on the other side of the hills, that was all tourist hype—he couldn't help but love the sound of that phrase: published author.

He had believed everything that MacMalcolm told him because he had been desperate to believe it. The first signs had been good. Liam knew all too well how many writers had been led down the garden path by moviemakers. But it was all legit.

The script was written. The first draft had actually been loosely based on Liam's most recent volume of war poems. Then it had been rewritten once, twice, three times, and each revision moved further and further from Liam's own vision and his own words until, at the end, there was nothing.

Nothing but his name and the fact that he was a soldier. He had tried to stop everything then, but MacMalcolm had persevered and flashed that promise of the poetry going into a book. They had had drinks at Spago with a big-time New York literary agent who'd vowed on her mother's grave it would happen, if the movie was made. So Liam had stifled his objections and signed the last of a long line of con-

tracts, this one promising to be the "technical adviser" on
the movie.

The final straw had been meeting Nick Falucci, and the
young actor's brand of posing and muscle flexing.

Liam got to his rented car in the studio lot. He took out
the keys and opened the door, climbed in and started up the
ignition. The Buick's wheels screeched in agony and protest as he powered the sedan out of the lot and onto the
freeway.

Liam was speeding down the freeway, weaving between
cars in a mad dash to get to the beach. The L.A. papers were
full of news about crazies who were taking potshots at driv-
ers on freeways. Well, Liam just wished one would try it,
any one. He was ready to do some cleaning up in the city
himself, and one of those idiots would make a perfectly fine
stand-in for MacMalcolm.

Liam gripped the wheel of the car hard. He needed the
ocean to calm himself. And he needed a good stiff drink.

He tore through downtown Los Angeles and through the
west part of the city, past the mansions of Beverly Hills and
Bel Air, and at last he could smell the Pacific.

When Liam had finally pulled off the freeway, he headed
for Venice Beach.

The old town was one of the strangest areas in Los Angeles. It was supposed to be a replica of the Italian city with
the same name, but the Depression had interfered with the
land developers' vision, and the pattern of canals had ended
abruptly. They had quickly been crowded with debris, and
the once grand plans had been scaled way back.

For years, Venice was a slum. It became a haven for
beatniks and then hippies. Compulsive bodybuilders lived
there now, close to their temple, Gold's Gym. They strut-
ted on Muscle Beach and posed for tourists. There was still
an artists' colony, and there was the ocean.

Liam parked the car and stalked along the boardwalk toward the house he'd rented for the duration of his stay in California. It was an old, overpriced structure with lots of charm and little else. The heat never worked, although the waterfront area could get chilly at night, and the appearance of hot water was sporadic at best. The rent was outrageous, because Venice was in the midst of being "rediscovered" by yuppies, which was the last thing it needed.

But the place was better than the sterile apartments that climbed the hills above Sunset Strip like mechanical dolls, all squared-off rooms with white plaster walls and postage-stamp-size swimming pools. At least Liam could see the Pacific Ocean through the windows of his house.

O'Toole composed himself a little bit more when he got to his own front door. There was no need to have Claude bear the brunt of his anger and frustration. When he thought he had himself under control, O'Toole sighed and then opened the door, which led directly into the living room.

"Hey, O'Toole, just in time!"

Claude Hayes, another member of the SOBs, had been rooming with Liam. He'd had little else to do during the layoff, and a vacation on the beach seemed just fine to him. O'Toole, as he always did, enjoyed having his friend's company.

"What are you doing?" Liam asked as he saw Claude throwing clothing into a suitcase.

"We got a job!" The big black man was all smiles at the idea. The idle time hadn't proved to be such a great vacation for him, after all.

O'Toole felt himself swell with joy. No more Hollywood! "Where are we going? When? How? Did Nile call? Is that it?"

Liam flew through the house and began to collect his own belongings. They still had three months of paid-up rent on the house, but O'Toole never wanted to come back. He wondered if he'd ever want to even come back to California in his life!

Claude stopped and studied his pal's fast reaction to the news. "Man, I thought you might be upset, having to leave your movie and all."

That was a lie. O'Toole had never admitted to Hayes just how much he loathed the whole scene, but the black man had understood it. He knew Liam well enough to have picked up the signs of discontent long ago.

The Irishman wondered if he should bullshit his friend, but he knew he couldn't do it. "Artistic differences," he said with a laugh.

"I just bet. You got the art; MacMalcolm has the differences. Well, get them behind you, my man, because we got a plane to catch to La Paz, Bolivia. We're going to see some mighty big mountains."

"Sounds good to me," Liam answered, and he meant it.

"I STILL SAY the Carib wouldn't have been pleased," William Starfoot II muttered, as if speaking to himself.

"What the hell are you talking about?" Alex Nanos asked sharply. He looked over to where the full-blooded Osage was sitting cross-legged on the prow of their rented yacht. How could anyone not be pleased with what they had going? Not only did they have a sixty-foot boat all to themselves, but they were also anchored in the harbor at Key West, Florida. They were in heaven! Who could think of any complaints?

The man whom all the SOBs called Billy Two looked back to Alex, who was sitting on a swivel chair attached to the aft deck of the boat. The big Greek had the latest of many gin and tonics in his hands and was happily bleary-eyed and already half-buzzed. It was only one o'clock in the afternoon.

Billy Two nodded to himself. "The Carib would be especially displeased with you."

"I don't even know who these jokers you're talking about are, Billy Two. Come on, give me a break. We're hard-working men on vacation. We don't have to worry about anyone."

"The spirits of the Carib are here, even now, in their sorrow at the sight of the degenerate white man," Billy Two intoned. "Their gods are defiled."

"Now you listen to me!" It was getting tiresome. Alex Nanos had been listening to Billy Two's newfound religion for weeks without complaint, but there was a limit. "I put up with you and that Hawk Spirit thing of yours, 'cause you're an Osage and that's your god and you think you've talked to him—"

"I *think* I've talked to him," Billy Two echoed with a negative emphasis, then stood up suddenly and clenched his fists. "I am one with Hawk Spirit."

"Okay, okay." Alex put a hand up in the air to try to chill out the big guy's anger. "You talk to him. I accept that. I know about all that stuff that happened in the South Pacific when we had that job out there, and I know all about how you jumped off the cliff and the Hawk Spirit-thing, he took hold of you and brought you to a safe landing in the water."

Alex took a drink of his gin and tonic before adding in a much lower tone of voice, "Of course, he also managed to let you break a few dozen ribs, bruise your insides and nearly kill you. But he didn't do that, I gotta admit. You are alive...as well as you're ever going to be."

Alex looked back up at Billy Two, who hadn't abandoned his pseudo-heroic pose on the deck. "Okay, you and that Hawk Spirit, I'll deal with that. But I am not going to take on all the gods of all the people in the world. I still don't know who the Caribs were."

Billy Two seemed to calm down a little bit. He moved toward the foredeck of the yacht, climbing down the short stairway until he was on the same level as Nanos. Alex watched the Osage approach him and studied the evidence of his pal's obsession.

Billy Two wouldn't even wear a regular American bathing suit anymore. He had some kind of loincloth on, something he'd created himself as a little symbol of his move back to nature. He had begun to let his hair grow long, and it was soon going to break on his neck. He wore an amulet he'd found in a tourist shop that claimed to deal with real artifacts of the Seminole Indians.

"You see, Alex—" Billy Two had arrived right by Nanos's seat and took the other chair next to him "—the Seminole, they lived on the Florida mainland. But the Carib, they were my brothers who ruled all the islands in this sea. That's how it got its name, get it? The Caribbean?

"So this island, Key West, was one of theirs. Now, I sit here and I look out at the cheap honky-tonks and the rip-off artists and all the fakes who come down here to do nothing but get drunk and spend money and razz women, and I know this isn't what my brothers, the Caribs, would have wanted to have happen to their homeland."

Billy Two, evidently happy to have made his point, stood up and went to the refrigerator in the galley. He opened the door and pulled out a can of Bud.

Nanos watched his friend with something close to awe. Billy Two didn't make the connection between what he'd just said and the fact that he was sitting on a million-dollar yacht and drinking pasteurized beer from an aluminum can. The man's wires didn't seem to meet. His elevator just wasn't making it to the top floor anymore, Nanos reminded himself again.

They had had too many conversations along the same vein to think that there was any reason to point out to Billy Two that he had become one of those tourists and that he was wasting time just like the rest of them.

What would he say if Nanos did confront him? He'd probably make up some bull story about his native right while still insisting that the other people were infringing on his people's land.

It was all too much for Nanos. He finished off his drink and got up from his chair, ready to move to the kitchen for another drink. He seemed to stumble a little bit as he moved. He didn't register that it might have something to do with how much alcohol he'd already consumed. Instead, he thought it was a slight problem caused by last night's intake of gin. It was, he was sure, the kind of problem that would best be handled by the hair of the dog that bit him.

Just as Nanos opened the bottle of good Tanqueray, the ship-to-shore phone on the boat sounded a distressingly loud ring. Anxious to stop the painful noise, Alex grabbed the receiver and lifted it up. "Hello."

The familiar and demanding voice of his boss, Nile Barrabas, came through the wire. "The International. La Paz, Bolivia. Two days. Room 1335. Be there."

"Nile, sure!" Nanos said, ecstatic to hear the one person who could end his strange vacation. "We'll be there with bells on!"

"Billy Two is with you, isn't he?" Nile asked.

"Oh, is he ever!" Nanos groaned.

Barrabas seemed to be taken aback by the answer. Then, a loud laugh told Alex that the boss understood. "Been having a few lessons in Native American folklore?"

"We'll talk, Nile," Nanos finished, then hung up the receiver and turned to look at Billy Two, ready to give him the news.

The Osage was looking out over the marina where they were docked. "There are too many undressed women here. It's unsightly."

"Well, we're getting out."

Billy Two turned quickly with a question on his face.

"That was Nile. We're going to Bolivia. There gotta be flights out of Miami. I'll call and make some reservations."

"The land of the Incas!" Billy Two answered, a little too enthusiastically for Alex's taste, and with that faraway look on his face that the Osage had displayed too often of late.

"The land of nose candy, that's all I know," Alex muttered in response. Then he turned to the phone and dialed information for Miami. He had to get out of there.

THE LAURENTIAN MOUNTAINS north of Montreal were just about as far from the climate, geography and life-style of Key West as anyone could imagine.

The Laurentians, though they do have some hydroelectric projects and some large-scale mines, are still one of the least spoiled parts of the North American continent. It was a place where a man with some money and a love of solitude could escape from the pressure of modern life.

Geoff Bishop had bought his spread many years ago and on it had constructed a large log cabin. At first glance, the rough building materials and the almost primeval state of the countryside around the house made his home seem very rustic. But when a visitor studied the layout more closely he saw that there were telecommunication disks carefully placed as unobtrusively as possible a few hundred feet from the main building. Those disks kept Geoff in touch with the world. He got the same satellite television programs that every other disk-owner coveted, but he also had access to the most modern and sophisticated communication systems in the world—even, in some cases, when the owners and users wouldn't have wanted him to.

Then, if the visitor were to look even more closely, he would see that the house was much larger than appeared at first glance. There weren't any other structures by which to gauge the scale of the building, for one thing. Without anything to compare it to, one saw merely a log cabin. Only a closer study of the structure revealed that the log cabin held three floors and that it had a state-of-the-art solar-powered heating system.

It wasn't a primitive cottage. Inside, the basic furnishings were surrounded by some of the finest art available from the auction houses of Europe. The building had more in common with the great hunting lodges that nineteenth-century millionaires had built in Maine and in the Rockies. It was the home of a very substantial man, one who could afford all the finest things in life, and who knew how to pick them out.

Right then Geoff Bishop was sitting in front of his fireplace, a huge hearth that could hold a ten-foot log. He was wearing outdoorsman's clothing and sipping a snifter of Napoleon cognac. Geoff was a sportsman, and that was why he'd chosen that isolated area in which to live. He wanted to be someplace where he could hunt, fish and mountain climb whenever he felt like it.

Though, actually, he mused while he tasted the sharp flavor of the brandy, it just might be that he was getting a little tired of all that.

Geoff got up from his comfortable chair and went over to look out the window. As much as he'd always respected the wilderness and had been careful not to damage the environment, there were some things that even a man like himself had had to do to allow him to live there.

The long line of asphalt that he could see was his big compromise. It was a runway for his private planes—a Lear jet for fast, long-range travel, a Piper Comanche for local hops and an old biplane, just for the hell of it.

Those planes were all in their well-camouflaged hangar. At any moment, he could walk out to the hangar and get in one of them and go wherever his heart desired. Living in isolation is a lot easier, he thought, when you knew you didn't have to stay there.

As beautiful as spring was in the Laurentians, he was thinking of just that—leaving his isolation. He studied the spectrum of greens that the new forest growth had shot up recently, thought about what a glory of nature they were, and then thought about ...

The phone rang, bringing Geoff back from his speculations. He sauntered over to the instrument. Calls to his hideaway were very infrequent, so infrequent that it never was worthwhile speculating about who a caller might be. Besides, sometimes there was a desire for a certain special person to be the caller and, if that expectation wasn't met, disappointment followed. Geoff wanted to keep his own private expectations down to earth.

"Hello," he said into the phone.

"Geoff, Nile here. We have an assignment."

Geoff broke out into a boyish grin and fought to keep the pleasure out of his voice. It was best to handle things in a very matter-of-fact fashion. "Good to hear it, Barrabas. Where we going this time?"

"Bolivia. The International at La Paz. Room 1335. The team's going to meet in two days. Any problem meeting that schedule?"

"You know, I'm going to miss fishing season up here," Geoff said, just to make sure he didn't sound too anxious at that particular moment.

"Your bank account in Switzerland will thank you," Nile Barrabas answered, clearly not worried about Bishop's recreation and reminding the pilot just how it was that he could afford the splendor of his Laurentian homestead.

"Yeah, the electric bill on this place is a killer," Bishop said, finishing up his own game.

"See you there."

Barrabas hung up the phone, but Geoff didn't replace his own receiver for the beat of a few seconds. He was grinning like a college kid now. Seemed like the team leader had just solved his social problems. He was going to get another date with Lee Hatton, and he didn't even have to ask the girl if she wanted to go to the prom. He knew she'd be there.

"*CARA*, WON'T YOU PLEASE have this dance with me?"

Lee Hatton looked at the man and smiled. She vaguely wondered if he realized he was a simple experiment for her. She doubted he was that smart. She didn't think anyone here was.

The couple moved to the center of the dance floor, and the Spanish—or was it Portuguese?—duke took her in his arms and they began to move across the floor. The eyes of most of guests at the Count de Marte's annual ball were on them.

Majorca, where Lee Hatton lived, was a center for high European society. She had known for years of the existence of that world, and she'd also known she could enter it whenever she wanted to. After all, she was the daughter of a famed American general, had attended the best schools in the States and, now at least, was extremely wealthy.

The family heritage—there had been other generals before her father—gave her the pedigree. And everyone assumed that the money was as old as the name.

That wasn't true. The family had relied on military salaries for too many years to accumulate any great amount at all. In fact, only a few years before Lee had been in danger of losing Casa Hatton, her "family seat," as social climbers liked to call it. Then the money had arrived—a lot of it.

She wondered vaguely what her Hispanic duke would think if he knew that the woman he was guiding across the floor of the ball was a mercenary. He would probably have enough trouble if he knew that she was a doctor.

Lee Hatton was an M.D. But it would be the image of the beautiful and worldly woman as a fighter that would probably really send the guests—fakes, she substituted in her mind—into orbit. She looked over the duke's shoulder and saw a gaggle of jet-setters from California watching her with obvious envy. They would have been glad to pay for the duke's company if they had to.

Of course, she realized with a smile, maybe they had. The duke's royal lineage was unquestionable and common knowledge, and so was his poverty. How he made the two of them fit together, gossip liked to say, had a great deal to do with his quick moves. He was as facile in the privacy of his bedroom as he was publicly on the polo fields.

She could feel the duke's hand making a slow descent over the small of her back. He's trying to make a move, she thought to herself in disgust. It was too boring, the whole thing was too boring.

After the past few years as the only female member of the SOBs—the mercenaries with whom she had trained and become a part of—Lee had no time or patience for the sham masculinity of part-time gigolos.

As the duke's hand made another sortie south of her waistline, Lee vaguely wondered what the crowd at that elite party would think if she were to calmly and effortlessly toss the duke over her shoulder. She loved the image—and the knowledge that it was entirely within her power to perform the move—and laughed out loud for the first time that night.

"*Cara*, what is it?" the duke asked.

She wasn't going to let him in on the vision she'd just had. The poor man's ego would be crushed by it, and there wasn't time to bother trying to put it back together.

"Nothing, your grace. But I am tired. I'd like to go back to my table."

"Of course, dear lady, and we'll have champagne!"

Lee realized she'd let herself be finessed. The duke had found a way to take her retreat and turn it into his own advance. So long as she wanted to play the society game, she'd have to do the proper thing and allow the gentleman to join her table.

But did she really want to continue all that foolishness?

Lee wondered about that question as she took her seat and allowed the duke to play big shot, ordering around the waiters. She caught the eye of one of them and realized it was Pedro, the second son of one of the peasant families whose farm was adjacent to her own house. She threw him a secret wink and got back a broad smile.

Lee knew that she would much rather sit with Pedro's family over a bottle of the local wine and talk about the problems of growing better olive trees on the difficult island of Majorca than where she was under the striped party tent.

Then, what game was she playing, she questioned herself. Pedro brought a bottle of champagne to their table.

The duke was bantering about nothing in particular while Pedro stood over her and poured her glass full of bubbling wine. She thanked him by name—surprising the duke by even noticing the young servant—and sipped her wine.

She was making a foolish attempt to go back and try out a kind of life she'd never known before, just to make sure she wasn't missing anything. The only child of a general, an almost too-brilliant student in college and in medical school, she'd never simply been . . . a girl.

Did she like any of it? She tried to answer the question as she considered the absurdly expensive designer gown she was wearing, the meaningless jabbering of the pretentious duke, the shrill and drunken laughs that came from the rest of the party, and she knew she didn't at all.

She looked up at Pedro and realized that of those present he was the only person she'd want to spend more than two minutes talking to. What did she want, then? She tried to block the answer: it was too obvious and easy. She wouldn't say the words. But the image of the Laurentian Mountains came across her consciousness anyway, and she was suddenly curious, wondering what Geoff Bishop was doing on his own time off.

Beep . . . beep . . . beep . . .

The sound steadily penetrated the party noises. The duke shut up, and the other guests who were seated nearby all looked up to try to find the source of the intrusive noise.

Lee leaped with glee for her bag, opened it and pulled out a beeper. She depressed the button to retrieve the message and heard the scratchy but unmistakable voice of Nile Barrabas, recorded on the answering machine tape and transmitted to her current location.

"Got a plane for you to catch. Call me."

"*Yo!*" Lee answered enthusiastically. An assignment! She was going to go out into the field with real people—who just happened to be real men, and they were going to do something instead of whiling away their lives on a dance floor, playing at being "society."

Lee couldn't restrain herself. She jumped up from her chair and kissed the duke on the chin, "Later, Charlie."

"My dear lady, what could be the meaning—"

The waiter must have understood just how bored Lee had been and how happy she was that she'd received the strange electronic message. He also must have known that, while the duke was hardly a real problem, he was about to become even more annoying than he had been earlier.

Pedro managed to nonchalantly tip over the full bottle of champagne he'd been carrying and let the well-chilled wine splash over the duke's crotch.

Even the remote idea of his very livelihood being frozen out of commission hurt the duke more than the physical discomfort. That, and concern with his elegant appearance, took all of his attention and kept him from caring about Lee's departure.

She was going to owe Pedro one for this, Lee thought as she rushed through the bushes that bordered the garden, managing to rip her new Lacroix original to shreds. It had once been worth thousands of dollars, but after a couple hundred yards sprinting toward the parking area, it wasn't good for anything but cleaning rags.

She didn't care at all. If she'd thought about the money, she would have realized that she was on the way to another half-million-dollar paycheck. But she would have been just as anxious to get going. What was really driving her was the knowledge that the team was getting back together again, and she'd be part of it one more time.

NATE BECK LIVED in a small house on the Connecticut side of Long Island Sound.

There was one thing that Nate loved. Computers. His mother had once said that when he first opened his eyes, he didn't grasp for her breast the way any other baby would, but began to study the surgical machines that were surrounding them in the hospital delivery room. His first smile hadn't been for her, but for an oscilloscope screen on one of the monitoring devices.

The man was born to hack.

He was madly unpacking the latest in a series of computers, which had just been delivered. It seemed that every computer manufacturer in the world was coming out with new products. The new Intel chips were opening whole new worlds to computer freaks like Nate.

In fact, he was more used to dealing with the big, big machines, the mainframes that were used to plan a whole nation's economy or the mammoth Cray machines that were capable of designing a continent's defense.

The new personal computers were mere toys for him. But what pleasure they brought!

He was so excited by the latest delivery that he almost didn't hear the phone ringing. When he did, he stood up and studied the instrument with intense distrust. There were evil forces out there in the world, and their best way of reaching him was by telephone. He wasn't at all sure that he wanted to give in to their deceit.

Those forces were his ex-wives and their mouthpieces, the lawyers of the world, the arrogant bastards who'd been given a law degree and who understood that the piece of paper wasn't any kind of academic achievement, not really. The truth was more blunt. A law degree was a license to steal. From Nate Beck.

Nate moved cautiously and anxiously toward the threatening phone. He'd have to answer. It might be someone else, after all, and not an attorney.

"Hello," he finally said very cautiously.

"I nearly gave up on you, Beck."

The boss! flashed the relieved thought into his mind. "Nile! How's it going? What's up?"

"An assignment in Bolivia. We rendezvous in two days at the International in La Paz. Get a flight out of Kennedy in New York as soon as you can. Here's a number. Try to make it in just one day, if you can, Nate. I need you early for some special consultations."

"Sure enough, Nile. I'll be there, no matter what. Even if I have to lease a plane."

And he meant it. Because, no matter that there was always danger on an SOBs assignment, going to Bolivia meant something else to Nate Beck as well. He'd be out of the country. The wives and their lawyers and their interfering courts couldn't get to him or his money. They could all stew, wondering where he was this time. And they'd never find out.

Going on assignment with the SOBs meant a stay of financial execution. Nate loved the idea.

5

Ole Bergson was still terrified, and Lennart Moberg was annoyed with his fellow Swede. Thousands of miles away from Stockholm and the scene of the crime, they had no reason to be worried any longer. They had made it. They had slipped out of Sweden with no problems and then easily made their way out of Europe to Bolivia.

It was to be their haven, and probably much more.

Ignoring Bergson's fidgeting, Moberg calmly retrieved their bags from the airport conveyor belt and then split the burden between them evenly. "Come on, then, Ole. We must get on."

"Yes, yes, of course," Bergson said too quickly. His small dark eyes continued to scan the crowds at the La Paz airport as they moved toward customs.

"This should have all been arranged," Moberg said, trying to soothe his countryman. "We'll have no problem here."

"I just wish I had a gun," Bergson answered.

Moberg looked at his companion again and couldn't suppress the smile on his face. It was highly unlikely that even a trained member of the Swedish police was going to get to carry a hand weapon on an international flight these days.

The criminal element is a terrible thing, Moberg thought to himself. The idea that businessmen could have their travel disrupted by outlaws was something that really offended the Swede. He would never have thought twice about the danger to tourists or innocent children. If children ever crossed his mind, it happened when he was disturbed by their screams in some public place where he felt they shouldn't be at all.

Lennart Moberg had never thought to consider himself a criminal. He was, so far as he was concerned, an entrepreneur. He was purely and simply someone who had identified a potential market, gone through the necessary steps to create a product for it and became involved with arranging the distribution of his product.

It had never registered with him that almost every country in the world would judge his enterprise as being highly illegal. For him, laws were simply something that were there to be avoided. They were the annoyances that leftist governments put in the way of businessmen like himself. Any right-thinking person would understand that, Moberg believed. No one who counted in the world would ever condemn him.

Besides, he had proof that in Bolivia, at least, his skills and his vision were appreciated by the people in power.

"Mr. Moberg, of course, General Valdez had told us to expect you." The customs official was suddenly all smiles after he'd studied the Swedish passport Moberg had handed him. The urge to give a good-looking, well-dressed blond European a hard time on his entry into this Latin country disappeared as soon as the bureaucrat understood that the man was somehow aligned with the powerful General Valdez.

The official reached over and took Ole Bergson's passport next. Even though it was obvious that there wasn't going to be a problem, Ole seemed anxious about surrendering his papers, as though they were the only thing substituting for his always dearly beloved and now missing weapon.

"*Señor*, please," the customs man said. His puzzled expression and his submissive tone of voice was evidence that he didn't mean to pose any threat to the Swedes. Still, it took another beat of time for Ole to hand over the passport.

"*Gracias,*" the official said, obviously relieved that the strange gringo didn't make life any more difficult for him.

Moberg assumed the man was actually frightened of them. They were under the protection of the all-powerful Valdez, and no minor cog in the works of the Bolivian government was going to interfere with anyone who had that connection. They why, he thought with great exasperation, wouldn't Bergson calm down?

"Everything is in order," the official said pleasantly after only glancing at Bergson's passport. He then marked their luggage with chalk—not even bothering to open it for an inspection—and bowed them toward the doorway leading out of the terminal.

The two Swedes went only a few steps past the customs area before a uniformed chauffeur approached them.

"Señor Moberg," he said submissively, "may I take your bags."

He smiled at the man and allowed him to carry his luggage. Good servants were difficult to find in the world today. Few Swedes or Americans or citizens of other rich industrialized countries were willing to assume such tasks anymore. It made Moberg all the happier when he did encounter a person who was apparently satisfied with the role.

They were led to a Lincoln stretch limousine that was blatantly parked in an illegal zone, but the many policemen in the area who were directing traffic weren't paying any attention to the vehicle.

They climbed into the enormous back seat of the Lincoln. Moberg hadn't had any liquor to drink on the plane. His experiences with the combination of the dry artificial air of the pressurized compartment and the way he knew human bodies were dehydrated from long travel over many time zones had taught him the danger of mixing alcohol and airplanes, but the trip was over.

The car had a fully stocked bar. He reached over and poured himself a light Scotch and soda. "Will you have something, Ole?" he asked his companion.

"Yes, yes. Vodka, just ice."

Moberg frowned as he poured the drink for the other man. Straight vodka wasn't a good sign, not at all. He'd watched disapprovingly Bergson's constant drinking during the trip, ignoring Moberg's advice that they not do so. He didn't need a drunk on his management team.

But it wasn't the right time to deal with that. He handed one glass to Bergson and sat back in the plush seat of the limousine with his own Scotch and watched the scenery speed by.

La Paz is at an altitude of 12,500 feet, making it the highest major city in the world. The air was thin, Moberg knew, and it was going to take some time to get used to the slight deprivation of oxygen. He'd have to watch himself and he'd have to especially watch Ole; alcohol's effect is dramatically increased at this elevation.

The Andes didn't seem as spectacular as when they had viewed them from the airplane. They were actually so very far up in the mountains that the sense of scale was thrown off. The scenery wasn't much different from the impression he had in many cities at much lower altitudes. They were only seeing the very peaks of the mountain range now; they couldn't see the vast valleys below and the steep climb that would have to be made if they had taken an overland route.

Lake Titicaca, the largest lake in South America, was nearby. It was a huge inland sea of vast depths, full of strange life, with fish species that hadn't been studied even by the most advanced university zoologists in the world.

When this is all over, Moberg thought to himself, and I am a multimillionaire, perhaps I'll look into creating an encyclopedia of Titicaca's splendors.

That seemed like a pleasant idea. Every good business-man dreams of retiring and using his free time and his fortune to help the progress of learning.

The limousine skirted the center of La Paz and drove directly toward an obviously wealthy residential area. It was a pleasant contrast to the approaches to other capitals of Latin America or Africa, where Lennart was forced to look at the distasteful poverty of the lower classes, who didn't care enough about their appearance to even bathe properly.

Though, Moberg suddenly remembered, this wasn't the official capital of Bolivia. While, in fact, the city housed all the administrative offices of government as well as foreign embassies, the legal capital of Bolivia was Sucre, a small city to the southeast where the supreme court was located.

It was just another minor bother that a country like Bolivia would provide to a foreigner such as Moberg, forcing him to go to an inland center for meaningless paperwork and an excuse for another bribe.

"I'd like another drink," Ole Bergson asked, his voice slurring noticeably.

"Of course. I'm sure you can help yourself."

Moberg watched the other man pour the clear liquid into the glass without bothering to freshen his ice.

"We're here, *señores*," the driver suddenly announced as he pulled into a driveway.

Moberg put down his still nearly-full glass of Scotch in a receptacle in the car's bar; Bergson downed the entire tumbler of vodka in his own hand.

The long limousine went up the long drive and came to a stop in front of a traditionally styled hacienda. The Swedes got out of the Lincoln after the driver had opened a door for them, and they looked at the imposing structure.

The one thing that Moberg did understand was that he wouldn't be going back to Sweden. That possibility was gone. He had made a calculated decision about his future and about the potential payment he could receive from certain investments as opposed to others, and he had recognized that his own path was clear.

The Gothic cathedrals of Sweden were going to become memories. The ancient castles that he had once dreamed of owning weren't going to be his. He wouldn't walk the narrow streets of Stockholm again.

He would be here, most probably, in this Hispanic country for the rest of his life, he thought as he studied the lines of the hacienda much more carefully because of that knowledge. He found them pleasing. The adobe was a boring material, a very pale yellow that appeared almost white, though the rough texture of the dried surface was interesting. The bright native tiles decorating portions of the doorways and the outline of the roof, however, showed some very interesting, if primitive artistry.

Perhaps I'll end up collecting them, he thought. A good businessman should also support the arts, especially in a case like this. Bolivia was so very poor that the native handiwork couldn't possibly cost much.

The chauffeur, struggling with their bags, led them into the hacienda.

The most amazing thing about the interior of the building was its cool air. The Spaniards who had colonized almost all of Latin America had been geniuses in devising ways to beat the pounding rays of the sun. Their knowledge of just how many windows a place could have and in what position they should be to fight the midday sun was amazing.

The tiles that had only been used decoratively outside were the major building material in the interior of the house. The bright hand-painted colors were even more impressive there.

Yes, Moberg thought as he walked across the hallway and listened to the leather soles of his shoes clicking against the hard floor, this will become very pleasant.

He remembered again his interest in the fact that he was actually in Valdez's house: he was witnessing the reality of the life of his new business partner. He rightly suspected that Valdez had simply taken over the building from some poor fool who had been caught in a cross fire between the many warring factions of Bolivian politics. Someone had bet his bribes on the wrong side of a revolution and, when he'd gone off to prison or before a firing squad, there had been no lack of a volunteer like Valdez to move into the abandoned home.

"Please, *señores*, make yourself comfortable. The general will be with you soon. I will take your bags to your rooms and unpack for you."

"Thank you," Moberg said politely.

"You stay the hell of out my suitcases!" Bergson said loudly. "I don't want any strangers going through my luggage."

"Well, of course, *señor*, if you wish," the man agreed, though he was obviously stunned by the outburst.

"Ole, he's not a spy. It's customary for servants in good homes to unpack for guests." Moberg could hear the annoyance build in his own voice. He was losing control over his reactions to Bergson, and Lennart hated losing control over anything.

"Not for me," Bergson muttered as he moved to the bar to pour himself one more drink. "I don't want any spic looking at my dirty underwear or stealing it or anything."

Moberg sauntered over to one of the couches, which were covered with a rough cotton cloth—another native handiwork, he suspected—and sat down. He studied the other Swede silently as the man downed a drink without hesitation and then poured himself still another.

"Does it really bother you?" Moberg finally asked him.

Bergson turned quickly and looked at Moberg with surprise. "The murder? Of course it does."

"It was only a means to an end. The man was going to expose us. Our time and effort would have been wasted, and we would have gone to prison. He had to be eliminated."

"He was the damned prime minister, Lennart." The way Bergson's voice drifted off as he continued to speak was the most telling part of the statement. "And there was the woman, his wife. She was innocent. She wasn't a part of all this. I thought it was so easy at the time. I was proud it had gone so well. But now, whenever I have dreams at night, I see the shock on her face, and that one quick moment when her mind registered just what was happening. Of course it bothers me."

Moberg looked at the man more carefully, as though he were suddenly a shockingly different form of life, a beast as strange as any he would ever find on the floor of Lake Titicaca. "You *do* care."

"I told you I do."

Moberg frowned and wondered what those emotions would feel like—guilt, regret, despair. He was trying them on for size, just in case he had to use them someday in his own life—though he couldn't imagine why he ever would.

Then his mind drifted to another point of view, and he speculated how such emotions might affect Ole Bergson's role as part of his team. Would they inhibit Ole's usefulness? he wondered.

"The general is here, *señores!*" the chauffeur announced.

Without really thinking, Moberg stood up and turned toward the door to greet Valdez. He regretted it immediately, thinking that he should have made the other man come to him, so Valdez wouldn't think that simply because they were in his country they were in any way under his power.

"Gentlemen!" Valdez said with Hispanic exuberance as he pushed through the portal, his arms outstretched to greet the newcomers. A quite beautiful young woman—his secretary? Moberg wondered—stood behind Valdez. He was flanked by his omnipresent bodyguards, two Bolivian National Guardsmen. Apparently they never left his side and had accompanied him overseas for the secret meetings with Moberg to plan the joint enterprise together.

Moberg tried to recall their names, then realized that it was a fruitless exercise. They were simply living guns to Valdez. That was how anyone involved with Valdez needed to see them. They carried their large, heavy American-made rifles with the ease of men who always expected to have weapons in their hands. Officers' Colt .45s showed in their waistband holsters, and sheathed beside the handguns were hideously large Bowie-style knives.

The two guards' appearances indicated they were of native stock. Their noses, and specifically the high foreheads of their Inca ancestors, were their most striking features. Nothing about them even hinted that the Spanish conquerors had deposited seed in their bloodlines. No, Moberg thought condescendingly, the primitive Indian genes dominated their physical attributes, and undoubtedly formed their mentalities, as well.

These men were probably the only two soldiers in the world whom Valdez trusted totally. They were surely operating from an ancient belief in loyalty that modern troops could barely comprehend. Lennart studied them as they stood at rigid attention by the doors and thought them very handsome consumer items. He'd like to buy something like them for himself one day.

Valdez, his arms still outstretched, was coming closer to Moberg. The Swede stiffened at the idea that the Bolivian might want to touch him and quickly shot out his arm for a handshake. The gesture served to ward off a more intimate touch.

The general seemed to be momentarily surprised, but cordially accepted the proffered hand. "You are very welcome here in your new country," he said with a smile.

Valdez and Moberg were actually two of a kind. Both were well-built men in their mid-thirties whom women would find attractive. Men would have sensed the effort they had each put into staying in shape. The fact that Moberg was so blond with a pale complexion and blue eyes while Valdez was olive-skinned with dark black hair and brown eyes didn't really detract from their similarities. It actually seemed to underline how alike they were, making them appear to be a purposely miscolored set of twins.

"And you, as well, Señor Bergson." Valdez moved to the now drunk Bergson, who wasn't in any condition to free himself from Valdez's bear hug.

"Thank you, sir," Bergson managed to say when Valdez finally released him.

"Now, you have all the refreshments you need?"

Moberg waved off the offer, while Bergson went directly over to the bar and topped off his vodka without even acknowledging the general.

"Yes, well . . ." Valdez said as he shrugged at Bergson's rudeness. He clearly didn't want to pursue the matter. "I have your new papers right here with me."

Valdez snapped his fingers, and his secretary came forward with a folder that the general took in his hands. Moberg looked at her more closely, and even more appreciatively. She was a very handsome woman, with pale skin and dark brown eyes of a traditional Hispanic beauty. He would have to discover if she was Valdez's private property, or if she was simply someone whom he might be willing to share. As soon as Valdez had taken the papers, the woman left the room. Her job was obviously done. The Swede watched the beautiful view of her firmly rounded buttocks as she departed. As much as he regretted her departure, he equally welcomed the resulting absence. He didn't want to have to deal with that kind of distraction just then.

"It's all here, and completely legal, of course." Valdez opened the file and was leafing through some papers. "You gentlemen will have to take an oath, sign a naturalization request. . . ."

While the Bolivian was talking, Moberg had moved toward the two men who stood guard at the doors. He looked at their rifles with interest. "These are M-16s, aren't they?"

"Yes," Valdez said. With a perplexed look that plainly showed he didn't understand what that had to do with anything.

Moberg extended his hand toward one of the M-16s. "May I?" he asked the general, who nodded to one of the soldiers. The simple nod was an obvious order, and the guard formally handed the M-16 to Moberg.

He studied the weapon with a keen eye. "I've never actually held one," he said conversationally. It was plain that he knew quite a bit about arms. He sighted the rifle from the front of the barrel backward, testing the metal, then turned the M-16 around and hefted it, gauging its weight and balance.

"You really should consider one of the new Swedish rifles, General," Lennart said. "Interdynamic AB has been testing a model they call MKR that uses a rimfire, high-velocity cartridge to great effect. When it goes into production, I predict it will become one of the best standard assault rifles in the world.

"This one, on the other hand, has given the Americans and their allies a great deal of trouble."

"The MKR might be interesting, Señor Moberg," Valdez said carefully, certain that the Swede was up to something he didn't understand. "But actually, the M-16s come to us almost free of charge. Now that my troops are doing such an effective job clearing the drug trade out of Bolivia, the fools in Washington have been very anxious to make sure they have the very best weapons readily available to them.

"The M-16 isn't that bad, in any event. You're probably thinking about the M-14, which was the rifle with the bad reputation because of the way it performed—or didn't perform—in Vietnam. There's a new model—the Mini M-14—which has proven very effective, and even the original model has had its drawbacks corrected."

"So this gun, this M-16, is an adequate weapon?" Moberg asked, his voice full of skepticism.

"Yes. It's the backbone of the infantry of almost every non-Communist country in the world." Valdez, suddenly bored with the game, waved in Moberg's direction. "Take it outside," he said, "try it out, if you insist."

"No, here will do."

Before anyone could understand what he was doing, Moberg had lifted the M-16 and caught Bergson in his sights. He pulled the trigger quickly, and a torrent of automatic fire ripped through the living room.

The hard tiles lining the wall made the explosive sounds of the rifle fire echo over and over again with increasing volume. Valdez dropped to the floor on his face, not even thinking about the reflexive action until the pain and blood coming from his nose finally registered with his brain.

Then he jumped up in horror from the reality of his own wounds, holding his nostrils tightly together to staunch the bleeding, while, wild-eyed, he surveyed the scene around him.

His bodyguards were battle ready. The one who still had his own M-16 had it aimed directly at Moberg, ready to fire if the Swede turned on them, especially General Valdez. The other guard had drawn his pistol and had assumed the grotesque and unmistakable marksman's stance: legs spread far apart, he held the weapon firmly straight out in front of him in a two-handed grip, his knees bent and his hips thrown back for more stability.

At one word from Valdez, Moberg would be dead. Feeling the warm seeping of his own blood between his fingers, Valdez was ready to give that very order. But then he watched as Moberg nonchalantly dropped the rifle on the floor, careful to do it while his back was still turned to the Bolivian guards, making sure they didn't suspect him of any interest in more foul play.

Moberg was smiling when he empty-handedly turned to face the general. "I'm so sorry for your accident. I suggest ice for the bleeding. It really does help, you know."

Valdez nodded slowly in answer. Two servants ran into the room just then, each of them wielding a Colt .45 similar to the guards'. It was very apparent that everyone in the Valdez household was prepared to do double duty. There was no place there for a man whose talents were limited only to domestic chores.

"Ice," Valdez yelled to them without taking his eyes off Moberg. "Buckets of ice."

The servants seemed to freeze for a moment, then they came suddenly to life and ran to fulfill the order.

Valdez moved over to where Bergson's body was sprawled on the floor. The look of shock was still on the dead Swede's face. He hadn't had even a moment to understand what was happening to him. Just as he'd assassinated the prime minister in a way that kept the politician from comprehending what had happened to him, so Bergson had died himself.

Bergson's mouth was wide open. A line of blood that had been thinned by his saliva was dribbling out of one side of his lips. His tongue had rolled lifelessly over his mouth, taking away any semblance of dignity the man might have had in his death. Valdez could smell the alcohol fumes that had soaked into the man's body, and there was a faint stench of urine. Like so many other men beset by sudden death, Bergson had emptied his bladder.

The .223 caliber bullets had cut through Bergson's body in an astonishingly straight line across his chest. Valdez squatted down on his knees, and his eyes traced the path of the bullet holes. He immediately realized that if Bergson's chest were bare, the indentations would have joined his two nipples together in a macabre kind of connect-the-dots game.

That couldn't have been done accidentally. Obviously, Moberg was a man who understood how to use a rifle.

Valdez stood up and looked at the places where the bullets had hit the tiled wall after having pierced Bergson's body. There were many chips in the enamel surfaces, and they all seemed to have a halo of discoloration from the red blood that had squirted out of Bergson's chest when the rounds had exited his body.

"I am sorry about that. Perhaps I can have them replaced," Moberg said.

Valdez turned to look at the Swede once again. Moberg had finally decided that it might be time to have a drink, after all, and was pouring himself an inch of cognac at the bar.

The general flicked a hand toward his two guards who, though not leaving the room, moved to a less threatening parade-rest stance. The servants came bustling back, each one with two full silver ice buckets. They also had clean white towels formally draped over their forearms.

Understanding exactly what they should do, they began to wrap ice cubes in the towels and to place them along the general's face to reduce the swelling and stop the flow of blood.

"Why did you do that?" Valdez asked, ignoring the ministrations the servants were applying to him. He was a man who was used to people paying attention to his body while he went on with his usual activities. There was no reason to wait to have that conversation any longer than necessary. "Why now?"

Moberg was moving his large-bowled brandy snifter between the palms of his hands, warming the cognac. He seemed surprised by the question and looked up. "General, in a matter of minutes you were going to make that man a Bolivian citizen, weren't you?"

"Yes."

"Well, wouldn't it have been much more difficult for you if I had killed him after that? Wouldn't it have offended your national pride? It had become clear that Bergson was going to be a difficulty and that he would have to be eliminated sooner or later. He had no more real usefulness for us. He helped me secure what we needed in Sweden and then he took care of the prime minister after that fool had become too interested in my research activities at the institute. But there was nothing left for him now. He was wasted baggage, and he was baggage that would have wanted some of our hard-earned money to be taken care of, as well.

"The course of action was clear to me. I have simply done it sooner rather than later to avoid some patriotic complications."

Valdez pushed away the servants, keeping one of the towels pressed against his nose himself. He stood there and looked at Moberg for a moment and then broke into astonished and gleeful laughter. "Oh, Lennart, my friend, we are going to be such good partners! We understand each other so very well!"

DINNER IN VALDEZ'S HACIENDA was a pleasant affair.

The steak wasn't done quite the way Moberg would have prepared it, but the sharp spices and the smooth taste left by the hardwood charcoal over which it had been grilled made it quite acceptable to him. The wine from the Sucre region was surprisingly good. It was a full-bodied red, rich and fragrant to Moberg's nose.

Valdez wasn't judging the wine—or anything else—with his nose right now. The bruises on his nostrils had made them swell up in an unsightly way. Moberg was really very sorry about that, but they had agreed to forgive and forget, even though that conversation had taken much longer than their discussion of the disposal of Bergson's rapidly decomposing body.

What made the meal especially pleasant was the presence of the beautiful secretary and the disclosure of her real role in the Valdez household.

"My sister is my right hand," the general had explained when they'd all gone to the table and sat down. "I have no mind for the details of administration other than those that have to do with the military, but Lucia has studied public affairs at the Kennedy School of Government at Harvard and has a wonderful grasp of such things."

Lucia Valdez hadn't even bothered to try to fake an innocent's blush when she heard her brother's praise. Instead, she stared directly at Lennart, her eyes locking with his and keeping him seemingly riveted while Valdez kept on talking.

"When we finish the...alteration of the regime here in La Paz, I expect Lucia to take a very central and very public role in our national affairs. I'm even thinking that she might make a better president than I, for the sake of the publicity value of a woman in office, if nothing else."

"Oh, really," Lennart responded, not breaking eye contact with the beautiful woman. If the guards of the Valdez household had been living testimony of Bolivia's Inca heritage, Lucia was equal proof that the Spaniards had been there and left their mark.

That unflawed pale skin looked even more perfect against the naturally black hair cascading over her shoulders and the delicate touch of red lipstick. Lucia was dressed fashionably, though not ostentatiously, in a dress whose high collar and tight fit combined the best attributes of discretion and sexuality at the same time.

"We'll be working closely together, Señor Moberg," Lucia finally said as she picked up her fork. "I look forward to it."

Moberg kept his own eyes on Lucia for a while longer. He seldom reacted to women sexually. A good body, an attractive face and a air of availability weren't enough of a combination to turn him on by themselves. There had to be something else in the mix to make the woman alluring. He had never really thought about the formula very much. When there wasn't any sexual interest in his life, he never noticed it as something wrong or as something he felt he needed to correct. But in the presence of the beautiful Bolivian, Moberg felt himself very much caught up in the erotic possibilities of the moment.

"What is the political situation?" he asked Valdez. Even when he was considering sex, Moberg wasn't about to lose his interest in the business at hand.

"There will be a coup soon. I'm almost inclined not to go through with it. The present government is harmless, and its facade of democracy makes the Americans comfortable. But leaving the current situation alone presents the possibility that some faction may become too nosy, too interested in military affairs. That would be very bothersome.

"My troops are infinitely loyal to me. I have carefully pruned the ranks of the officer corps and have made some strategic transfers of battalions to assure that my own command is in residence around La Paz.

"The money has been...procured for other purposes, obviously—" Valdez smiled "—but no one suspects its true resting place. I do want to make sure there isn't any sudden desire on the part of our politicians to investigate its path. A revolution has many different causes, Lennart, and the justification for this one is as good as any other I know of."

Valdez paused to give his next words their due weight. "It will happen tonight."

"Tonight!" For once, even Moberg was taken aback.

The general shrugged. "It's a good time, trust me. I've planted stories in the press about the current regime and its alliance with the Americans. I've made sure that United States' payments that were to go to the peasants of the Chapare haven't reached their destination, and the peasants believe me when I tell them they've been diverted into private pockets here in La Paz.

"When my troops circle the presidential palace tonight, there will be nothing to stop them, certainly not public opinion.

"With that, our own activities can enter into their next stage." Valdez calmly put a large chunk of steak into his mouth and began to chew it. He was obviously amused by the conversation and the circumstances. Then he took time for a big swallow of wine before continuing talking to Moberg. "My friend, have you ever seen a revolution?"

"No, no, I haven't." Moberg smiled back at the Bolivian. "I'm sure they can be very amusing."

"Indeed. You'll have to see ours tonight."

6

The revolution as spectator sport, Moberg thought with a sense of amusement as he sat in the comfortable chair perched on the terrace of Lucia Valdez's apartment, high up in a building from where they could see the plaza before the presidential palace. He was sipping champagne from a crystal goblet. Beside him was Lucia Valdez, dressed for the occasion in a formal gown. Her beauty was wonderfully set off by the red satin of her dress and by the blood-red ruby that hung from a pendant around her neck to rest just at the point where the visible cleavage of her breasts began.

The jewel seemed to perform a conjurer's trick on Moberg, enticing him to study the two mounds of soft flesh. His gaze searched the satin-covered expanse with much more intensity than he would ever usually give to a woman's body. He felt as though he were being slightly vulgar, an emotion he didn't usually notice in himself.

"This is, after all, my country now." He smiled at Lucia as a proof of his sincerity. He'd taken the oath of allegiance to the republic of Bolivia less than an hour before. The naturalization papers were still in his suit jacket's inner pocket. "I think it's only right that a patriot take part in the affairs of his nation."

"Or course, Señor Moberg," Lucia answered, equally enjoying the humor of the moment. "Ah, look, here come the tanks!"

There was a rumble of metal against metal as the wheel treads of the American-made M1s ground against the concrete of La Paz streets. The city had been strangely quiet up till then, as though the entire populace had understood that the government was going to fall.

The citizens of La Paz had become geniuses in anticipating the alterations of power in their home city. Bolivia hadn't had a stable government since before the Second World War. Only a very, very few dictators had managed to stay in residence in the presidential palace for more than a year in the past four decades. The current occupant had been in his place for precisely six months, not a bad showing according to those who kept count.

Generally, revolution is a trial for any state to go through. It is usually a trauma for the body politic of any nation to have a violent exchange of power. But for Bolivia and a few other Third World nations, a change in government had become such a common event that it inspired no more interest than the change in the seasons. To many people it sometimes seemed that some things were around to stay in these countries, and graft, corruption, violence were among them.

What could a folk do in a situation like that? Sit out the worst of it, hope the losers understood their plight soon enough so they wouldn't try to be too heroic and endanger the civilians, and wish that the new rulers were not too cruel.

The tanks were coming closer with a growing rumbling. Lucia reached over and picked up the magnum of champagne that had been cooling in its bucket and poured herself some of the sparkling wine. Moberg had barely touched his own and waved away her offer of more from the bottle.

"Alfonso Martinez—the man who had been president of the republic until just about now—was a nice fellow," she said in an even, conversational tone. "He might have lasted a bit longer if he hadn't given in to some of the complaints of the landowners in the Chapare and El Beni. They thought they should receive more compensation for turning over a few pitiful acres to the peasants in those areas as a part of the land reform the Americans were demanding in exchange for their foreign aid.

"But Martinez was a fool, and he didn't understand that the landowners weren't very important in the scheme of things anymore. The peasants must be on the side of the government—Perón understood that in Argentina when he ruled. If the masses *think* you are a good person, they'll never turn on you, but on the middle classes.

"My brother understands these subtle elements of government, Señor Moberg. That is why I think he may actually be able to rule Bolivia for a substantial period of time.

"There! There he is!"

Lucia quickly stood up and suddenly seemed to undergo a remarkable transformation. Her previously pale cheeks filled with color, and her breasts heaved with excitement. "He's standing in the turret of the first one—do you see?"

Valdez was plainly visible in the M1 tank leading the line of armored vehicles up the broad avenue. The Bolivian general was wearing a chest-load of medals, a clear indication he didn't really take the battle at all seriously. In real combat, an officer dresses in a uniform as inconspicuous as possible, otherwise he would attract the enemy's fire. The opposition would be all too happy to remove the foe's leadership in the middle of a battle.

"He is so wonderful! This is his moment!" Lucia shouted.

The Swede was intrigued with her sudden display of passion. Was it her brother who evoked it, or simply the idea of witnessing war? He studied her intently, with a cool look on his handsome Nordic face. The answer to his question could prove exceedingly interesting—whatever it might be.

MANUEL NEGARA, TOO, had heard the tanks approaching. But the captain of the presidential bodyguard didn't think the sound of metal on concrete was an occasion for celebration. Far from it. From deep inside his chest came a profound and silent cry of agony: Not now! Not again!

The soldier in Negara wouldn't let simple emotions take over his response to the situation, though. He was a professional army officer with a job to do, and he knew he must do it right.

"Go to *el presidente* and get him up onto the roof," Negara barked to his second-in-command. "Call the air force bases and find General Lopez. He should still be loyal. Tell him to get a helicopter to the landing pad on the roof. Pronto!"

"Sir!" The lieutenant saluted sharply and then turned and ran to carry out his assignment.

President Martinez had been the best hope in years for democracy's return to Bolivia. He had been fair and just in his approach to the country's economic and financial problems. His land-reform program hadn't been revolutionary enough for many, but it was the most far-reaching and realistic that had ever been put forth in the country. The landowners who controlled huge tracts would have been compensated fairly in return for turning over small plots of farmland to the peasants, who would then, finally, have had a chance to become self-sufficient.

The Bolivian economy was in desperate need of that shot in the arm. Everything in the country had been going bad—other than coca. The tin mines that a century earlier had made Bolivia rich in the manner of California gold were useless now. High technology had produced plastics and new metal alloys that made tin worthless. Hundreds of illiterate miners, untrained for any other work, had swollen the ranks of the hard-core unemployed.

The richest farmland had gone unexploited for the most part. The peasants who were producing edible foods or crops such as flax, which could be either refined in Bolivia or else exported, were clustered around the shores of Lake Titicaca, while the much more fertile and more plentiful acreage in the southeastern provinces was left untouched or else used only for wasteful cattle grazing.

Martinez had at least begun to address those issues. And he'd begun to stop the endless cycle of waste and corruption caused by the cancer that was cocaine.

The millions of American dollars that could be earned by exporting that lethal drug to the United States had eaten away at whatever pride and dignity the Bolivian armed forces still had. Negara had watched his fellow officers succumb, one after another, to the huge bribes available from the drug manufacturers and dealers. He'd also watched the simple and honest people of Bolivia be lied to and misled by those officers.

There had to be an end to the cycles of degradation that were eating away at Bolivia like a national cancer. There had to be!

The first place to try to end it was right there, and right then. The tanks that were approaching had to be under the command of Valdez. Negara had kept an eye on the reports of troop transfers coming into the presidential palace, and he knew that someone at army headquarters had been shilling for Valdez, arranging for his followers to be in control of the army posts closest to La Paz. But he'd misjudged Valdez. The general had begun to move much sooner than Negara and his friends had thought possible.

"Get out the missiles," Negara ordered another of his lieutenants.

That would at least make this very interesting, Negara thought with a smile. He'd be damned if the president of the republic was going to go down without a fight.

The lieutenant and his men had rushed to the basement of the palace where Negara had secretly installed a battery of TOW hand-held antitank missiles for just such an occasion. There weren't nearly as many of the things as Negara would have liked, but there were enough to do damage to Valdez and his troops, especially since the general probably was expecting the palace to fall without a fight.

Valdez wasn't nearly so smart as he thought he was. He might have moved large numbers of his loyalists into positions where he could utilize them well, but those were illtrained infantrymen. Negara had done exactly the same thing in selecting the men who were members of the presidential bodyguard. The one difference was that Negara's men were the elite forces of the Bolivian National Guard.

The men had been drilled over and over again in upcoming procedures. A secret chain of command had been established, with loyalist members in each of the Bolivian armed forces. There was a cadre in the air force that was unswervingly loyal to the president and to his democratic ideals, just as the troops in the palace itself were. The small navy that Bolivia maintained on Lake Titicaca was also strongly supportive.

It had long ago been decided that a presidential escape by air or land—if it came to that—would be the most difficult and would leave the president too vulnerable to capture or assassination. But Titicaca was an international body of water. On the opposite shore of the lake was Peru.

Until well into the twentieth century, Bolivia had had its own outlet to the Pacific Ocean. An ill-advised war with

Chile had deprived it of its only seaport and of any good reason to have a navy. But traditions die hard, especially when they're connected with hurt national pride. Suffering from that defeat, Bolivia had demanded of itself a naval presence of some sort. If it couldn't be on the Pacific, then it would be on the expanse of Lake Titicaca. There were fast gunboats and cutters available to Negara and the president, which were part of that large force.

The helicopters that were to land on the palace roof would fake a rush to the border by air, but one, in fact, was to slip away to the lake and deliver the president to a waiting waterborne craft.

At least, if the worst came true, there could be an honest government-in-exile, one that would prick the consciences of the rest of the world's governments and lobby effectively for a revitalization of Bolivia. There would be a real opposition in existence. Negara had sworn it would happen, and he meant to keep his oath.

His men came running back up from the basement with their loads of deadly TOWs. Taking their places at the huge ceremonial windows on the first and second floors of the palace, they waited with the agony of the soldier about to do battle. They waited for their foe to come on the attack, waited for the bloodletting of war to start.

Negara moved behind one of his men and saw the line of M1 tanks forming a circle in the plaza. He could count at least twenty-five of them. They were all flaunting flags and ribbons, as though on parade, not going about the business of removing the government they were supposed to serve.

Negara swore impatiently under his breath. "I swore I saw Valdez in the lead vehicle earlier, but now that they've moved into that formation I can't tell for sure which tank is his. Forget it. It would have been sweet to knock him off at once and perhaps end this entire thing, but we can't wait any longer.

"Sight the tank nearest to us, that one there." Negara pointed so his man could see the target he meant. "Blow it away and let's show them what they're really up against."

The soldier smiled at his commander and nodded. With the barrel of the TOW he cracked the glass of the window, then stuck the barrel through the opening he'd created. Hefting the TOW on his shoulder, he brought the closest tank into the cross hairs of his missile's sights. He fired.

The TOW shot through the night air and burst on impact with the M1. The explosion ripped open the tank's tough steel skin. Negara watched and waited to see if any of the three-man crew inside would escape and saw some of his troops lift up their M-16 rifles in readiness. But before an escape was possible, the flames from the TOW's combustion reached the gasoline tank.

There was a *whoosh*, and the plaza was suddenly illuminated in the bright light of the intense, chemically-fed fire.

The line of M1 tanks froze, as though they were living beings caught in an unexpected catastrophe and shocked into inaction by the surprise.

The turrets of the tanks didn't budge. Evidently the men weren't able to get their orders, and the contingencies they'd planned for hadn't included a counterassault of that magnitude.

"More!" Negara screamed to his men, who were cheering the first hit. "Get more of them!"

A barrage of missiles flew out the windows of the presidential palace. Some missed their targets and others weren't well coordinated, with too many of the TOWs striking the same tanks, but the damage they did do was spectacular.

One after another, six of the M1s burst into flames from the missiles. Each one produced a second explosion when its fuel erupted.

The light in the plaza was so bright it might have been daytime out there. The fires roared, and flames shot up into the air. This is real battle! Negara thought to himself. I haven't been one of those fools who simply give up when a dictator approaches the front gates and demands surrender.

Negara watched as some of the tanks moved into a battle formation. A few of the rebels had found their backbone and their senses. They had recently been armed with the latest American 120 mm smooth-bore guns, cannons that weren't to be fooled with.

Two of the tanks roared and spit fire just then. The shells went slamming into the second floor of the palace, and the explosions of the heavy artillery shook the thick, well-constructed walls of the building, sending clouds of smithereens into the air.

"Fire your missiles!" Negara ordered.

A volley of TOWs streaked toward the offending tanks, but caught only one with a trio of missile explosions so intense the fuel was consumed in the initial eruption, not waiting that split moment to appear to be a separate, second eruption.

Just then Negara heard the sounds of the Hueys approaching the palace. That was the real victory. The air force was going to come through in time! His role was to hold off Valdez and to allow the president a chance to escape. It was happening. He was going to win!

The men under Negara's command cheered again, ignoring the onslaught of a more ferocious round of tank cannon fire at the palace. They knew what was happening and how important it was.

Another shock wave struck the palace as more of the M1s let loose with the 120 mm cannons. "Get the bastards!" Negara yelled at his men.

All of them moved so quickly and so efficiently that the next volley of TOWs seemed to have been synchronized. Their aim was more effectively spread out, as well, and there were four more tanks on fire in the plaza.

"I got them, Captain!" one of the men screamed victoriously. Negara looked over and remembered that the young soldier's name was Federico. He was no more than twenty years old, a youngster from a tin-mining region not far from La Paz, one of the poor workers whose hope for the future had been with the president's reform policies. Federico was someone whose heart was in the battle.

Just as Manuel Negara returned the soldier's smile, a blast of 120 mm fire roared through the building, and on their own first floor. The tank gunners had finally realized the source of their danger and redirected their fire.

Manuel was stunned into silence when the dust settled. Where Federico had once stood there was nothing, nothing at all. A gaping hole had appeared in the wall of the palace. The captain moved toward the scene, searching for the youngster's body, at least.

"Captain! Quick! The helicopters have landed and they're waiting for you!" One of Negara's aides was tugging at the commander's arm and repeating his name in a bid for attention.

"No! My men have been dying here. I will not abandon them!" Negara couldn't believe that there was absolutely no evidence that Federico had ever lived in the palace. He was lifting up pieces of rubble, trying to see if the young man's body was hidden beneath some of the stone and concrete debris. Perhaps he was still alive!

But the aide wouldn't give up. "Captain, the president needs you with him. The republic needs you alive." Small arms fire was whistling through the hole in the wall, and Negara was in real danger from the snipers who were advancing on the palace quickly, using the tanks as cover while they took aim at the defenders inside the building. Many of Negara's men had taken up their M-16 rifles and were returning with their own marksmanship.

"Captain, you must listen! You know the best soldier recognizes the time for retreat. It's now! Your men have witnessed your bravery, and they will not forget your courage. But they all know—*we* all know that you must leave. The regime in exile cannot go on without your help! It's time to let Valdez have his moment. You will return."

Negara saw the attackers' M-16 rounds ricocheting through the corridors. Another blast of cannon fire opened yet another breach in the palace walls.

Growling his displeasure, but knowing his aide was right, Manuel Negara began to hurry toward the stairway that would lead him to the waiting helicopters and, hopefully to safety. Once he'd reached the stairs, he started to run. When he was at the very top, a new explosion shook the building and another portion of the walls collapsed into rubble.

He turned around and surveyed the battlefield that had once been the symbol of Bolivian hope.

He made a silent vow: You're right—I will return. Then he bolted up to the rooftop of the palace to his waiting escape.

"IT WASN'T AS PRETTY as your brother might have hoped," Lennart Moberg said to Lucia when the fighting at the palace was finally over.

The still-smoldering shells of more than a dozen tanks littered the plaza. There were reports of similarly fierce resistance in other sectors of La Paz. Even then, early in the morning hours, they could hear the echoes of gunfire in the distance.

Lucia turned to him with a strange smile on her face. "But wasn't it more magnificent this way?" She clasped her arms around her upper body as she and Moberg still sat on the terrace. A shiver of excitement seemed to surge through her body. "It was so much more wonderful this way than it would have been if they'd just marched in unopposed."

"But that's obviously what the general had hoped for," he said. He was smiling at her, loving the way the flames from the tanks down below sent moving shadows over her skin, its paleness a perfect backdrop for their eerie red hues.

Lucia shrugged, unconcerned. "But it was so manly, to have fought a real battle this way." She turned to look at him. "You must understand that. You killed that man today yourself."

"A necessary move," he said.

"But you killed a man today," Lucia repeated, her voice rising with passion, and the passion had nothing to do with fear for reprisal for what Moberg had done. "You shot him down in cold blood. The guards told me all about it, as did my brother."

He returned her gaze and saw clearly at that moment what she was. There had been many hints and there had been suggestions over the course of their conversations, but he hadn't dared to press to find out if his suspicions were true. Now he knew they were.

She was a woman for whom blood was the final aphrodisiac. The battle scene that had become more complex than any of them had expected had touched her as no mere erotic foreplay could have.

Moberg made his move. He reached over and only barely touched her bare forearm. Lucia seemed to tremble at his touch. "I did fire that gun, and he isn't alive any longer," he said quietly.

"You watched it?"

"I saw it," he answered, not letting her arm go.

Lucia closed her eyes and moved her face closer to his. Moberg knew that if he kissed her, he could have her in every and any way he wanted. He smiled at her unseeing gaze and leaned forward, letting their lips meet softly.

As soon as the contact was made, Lucia's tongue shot out and invaded his mouth. There was none of the gracious and well-educated lady about her now. Her demanding intrusion was an expression of raw hunger, as basic as any woman's could ever be.

Lennart pulled back and ignored the hurt moan that escaped from her. He grabbed her arm more roughly and dragged her up from her seat. "There's no one else here now. Just us. Your brother's well; we've seen him from here. He'll stay with his troops for a while to survey the damage."

"Yes" was all that Lucia could say.

Moberg smiled and began to pull her back into the apartment. She followed docilely, not having the energy to struggle against him even if she had really wanted to.

He pushed her up against the bed and then forced her onto it. He leaned over and took hold of the neck of her gown. With one motion, he ripped it open, exposing her white breasts and their dark red nipples, already hard with excitement.

"Hurry, please, hurry," she said in a strangely raspy voice. "I can't wait, please, hurry...."

He stood there for another moment, studying the exquisite body in front of him with the greatest appreciation. He understood her, and she was going to learn to understand him. She expected him to simply continue to undress her, and she tilted up her pelvis in an invitation for just that. The slight movement made her look suddenly cheap, even slutty. He thought he could treat her that way if he wanted to, but he immediately knew that wouldn't be the manner with which he would handle her.

Moberg reached down to touch himself instead and then slowly let his zipper slide open. He reached inside his pants to bring out his hard flesh. It was going to be difficult to prolong the act of consummation, but he knew he had to make things last as long as possible.

It was their first time together, but it was only a beginning. Lennart Moberg thought he was falling in love.

7

Nile Barrabas looked out the window of his thirteenth-floor suite at the International Hotel in La Paz. The city spread out beneath him seemed strangely empty of people. There was no sign of activity that usually brought life to the international metropolis.

Not that Nile was surprised.

The causes of the ghostly appearance of La Paz were very apparent. There was evidence of warfare and destruction scattered all over the cityscape.

It wasn't what he'd seen in Vietnam, nor what an earlier generation had seen during the Second World War. In both of those theaters the devastation of modern war had left vast sectors of much larger urban areas as barren as the satellite pictures of the surface of the moon. In the Bolivian capital the testimony of armed conflict was more subtle.

Although there weren't entire blocks of burned rubble where buildings had once stood, the streets were dotted by smoke-darkened storefronts here and there. There were also too many shutters on the facades of stores that would have been doing a brisk business at that time of day in normal circumstances.

A number of abandoned cars were strewed around the streets. Nile knew that automobiles were the most common skeletons found after urban warfare. When cars were caught in cross fire between troops shooting live ammunition, their gasoline tanks became extremely vulnerable. A single stray bullet, red-hot from the explosion that had sent it catapulting through the air, could ignite the fuel in a split second and turn the automobile into an inferno.

The war was over, though. Nile was only witnessing the relics of the scattered fighting that had rocked La Paz just before his arrival.

It bothered him, and he knew just why. When a man plays a complex game of strategy—chess, say, or bridge—he can never assume that his opponent is making only one move for which he has to watch out. Simpler games let a player take everything that happens at face value, but a brazen series of assaults and retreats on the part of a master at chess may be camouflage, something to keep the opponent's attention away from the true action.

The kind of war with which Nile and the SOBs were involved was strategy at its more complex level. He was there to lead his forces in a very straightforward operation: find and destroy a cache of Bolivian cocaine, probably under control of some corrupted segment of the country's military, and then remove the enemy's ability to replenish their supply.

The revolution that had taken place in La Paz was probably just "noise" in his task—something irrelevant to what he was supposed to do. They could ignore it. Almost every other mercenary team in the world would. They would see the scars of destruction and shrug, then move into the jungle where the coca was grown and forget everything that had happened in the city.

But the other mercenaries of the world weren't the SOBs, and the SOBs wouldn't be so foolish that they would overlook the situation, and that's why they were the best in the world.

Barrabas turned away from the window and looked over at Nate Beck who was furiously working at the keyboard of his Compaq III computer. The tiny machine, which weighed less than twenty pounds, was equipped with the new Intel chips. Beck had worked out a way to utilize technologies with it that the buying public didn't even know about yet—and wouldn't for a number of years.

The keys clicked very softly as Beck worked away. Around him were books and computer printouts and charts of aerial surveillance done by American spy satellites that had been studying Bolivia on special orders from Washington.

Beck sat back in his chair and sighed. He looked over at Nile, and his fatigue melted away to be replaced by a sense of great satisfaction. The members of the SOBs liked nothing better than coming through when their leader asked them to take on an assignment.

Nate theatrically waggled a finger, and knowing he had Barrabas's undivided attention, slowly moved it to the Enter key on the board. He depressed it, and Barrabas moved over to watch the back-lit screen of the computer as it seemed to flash through thousands of different images in a matter of seconds.

Then the screen froze. It displayed columns of indecipherable numbers and other characters that meant nothing to Barrabas. But they didn't have to. That was why a good leader has specialists on his team. Beck knew precisely what they meant, and he translated them immediately.

"It's impossible. It is simply impossible that—given climate, soil conditions, water table levels, you name it—that Bolivia has another area that is capable of producing amounts of coca equivalent to the crop it's lost because of the buy-out of the Chapare.

"Assuming the data is correct," Beck added quickly. "That's the whole thing about any computer calculation, Nile: the data must be correct."

Barrabas shook his head slowly. He wasn't surprised by any of it, but he had wanted to have a second opinion from his own man. He and the rest of the SOBs had learned long ago never to trust the analyses that came out of the CIA. Langley, Virginia, the site of the headquarters of the United States Central Intelligence Agency, was the center of some of the worst bureaucratic incompetence they had ever encountered.

"Good enough. We're going to have to do some detective work, then. The cocaine is coming from someplace. There's no doubt the flow has been sustained even while so very many acres of land have been defoliated."

"They're pulling defoliation!" Beck said. "That seems to be a pretty heavy response, Nile. Hell, we saw what that can do in Vietnam."

"We sure did. The big crop-dusters come across and lay their blanket of chemicals over the jungle and...there's nothing left. It's a sure death for a forest. By the time the chemicals are done, there's no hope for new growth ever developing."

"I hate that kind of thing, Nile. I got these pictures in my head of all those guys who were caught by Agent Orange, as soon as you said that."

"They claim the new chemicals are better, less likely to affect humans. I sure as hell hope so."

The two men were silent for a minute. They both knew what was in the other's mind. Nate wasn't the only person who would think about Agent Orange the minute defoliation was mentioned. There were possibly thousands of troops who had been in Southeast Asia when the Pentagon had decided that it was the best way to stop the flow of matériel coming down the Ho Chi Minh Trail from North Vietnam, smuggled out of sight of the American air forces because of the thick tropical growth of Vietnam's forests.

The chemicals had been used without thorough testing and without serious concern that the troops exposed to them would ever be contaminated. But they were, and the legacy of that program had been strange cancers, unexplained leukemia, shortened life spans for a lot of good men.

"Why that, though?" Nate finally broke into their private thoughts. "I don't understand why that would work here, really."

"You've been working with the facts and figures. The Chapare isn't worth using for other crops. The officials in Washington pressed the Bolivians to use this method to make sure that coca wasn't grown there. It can't be grown there now, not in the areas they've sprayed.

"They're relocating the peasants to other parts of the country and hoping that the natives in the jungles survive."

"Blast it, Nile, I hate talk like that. They 'hope' the natives survive." Nate shook his head slowly for a moment and then came quickly back to life. "Holy hell, Nile. Don't you ever dare tell Billy Two what's going on! Do you know how that man will react if he hears that Washington is out to stifle the way those natives live? There will be hell to pay. Can't you just see it?"

"Yes—" Barrabas grimaced "—I sure can."

As if in answer, there was a sharp knock on the suite's door. Nile went over to open it, and there was William Starfoot II himself.

"Boss!" The big Osage dropped his luggage and his hands came up and grabbed Nile's shoulders. "This is one dynamite assignment. Hawk Spirit is *very* glad that I'm here!"

Alex Nanos was behind Billy Two, who now burst into the room and gave Nate Beck his own dose of excited greeting. Nanos didn't say a word. He simply gathered up Billy Two's suitcase and shoulder bag and carried them past the open door. He was obviously a victim of silent suffering.

"Good flight, Alex?" Nile asked as he shut the door.

Nanos threw his load onto the floor and turned to look at Barrabas. "He's talking to the Incas already. We flew over some of their ruins—over on the Peru side—and he damn near jumped off the plane. The fool thought his Hawk Spirit would catch him if he jumped out of a 747."

"I was just perking up the Greek's tired journey," Billy Two said from the background. "I wasn't going to jump at all. It was good to get the stewardess's attention, though. You gotta admit, Nanos, that worked."

Nanos wasn't going to be distracted from the reality of his tale. He didn't look over his shoulder to confront Billy Two face-to-face, but he raised his voice just to make sure everyone knew to whom he was talking. "Did you or did you not say you were talking to Hawk Spirit while we were in that plane, huh?"

Billy Two stood straight, bringing himself to his full height of well over six feet and throwing back his shoulders to assume all the dignity of an Osage warrior he could muster. "I spoke to Hawk Spirit and asked him about the gods of this place and whether there were any who were his relatives."

No one spoke. Billy Two studied the back of Nanos's head for a short while and only then looked from Barrabas to Beck. He was about to ask them if they believed him or not, but then decided not to make Hawk Spirit go through the indignity of having his very existence questioned.

"I have something from him. I think it's important you know this." Billy Two crossed his arms over his chest, warrior style. He was entering into the self-consciously Indian phase of his that he had moved in and out of since he had been captured by the Russians a few years ago. They had injected him with psychedelic drugs—besides sulfuric acid—trying to break him and get hold of whatever useful intelligence he could give them.

The Osage had survived the ordeal by reaching into the deepest parts of his past—and the past of his people. Nanos and others would always be convinced that the drugs had simply fried his brain to brittle bits, but Billy Two and a very few believers were convinced the whole ordeal had produced a profound religious experience.

"The gods of the Incas are angry. They've been forgotten and neglected. But their powers aren't to be feared. They've grown weak since the Spaniards came and sucked their believers away from them.

"But Hawk Spirit says that there are gods in the jungles who are fierce. They've seen the way the Incas—once the mightiest of the mighty—have fallen, and they will not have that happen to them and their people.

"The jungle gods..." Even while he spoke, Billy Two seemed to move away from the other men—not physically, but the look in his eyes and his tone of voice indicated that mentally he was going to another place somehow. "The jungle gods manifest themselves in the animals of the wild. They are most vicious when they take the body of the jaguar."

Billy Two appeared to become fully conscious of the other men, almost as if he had come back to earth. He looked around the group, as though puzzled by something, or frightened.

"The jaguar is almost the only beast on earth who hunts human beings for food."

"What the hell do you mean?" Nanos said quickly, turning around to look at Billy Two.

"Just what he said," Barrabas answered for Billy Two. They all looked over at him, surprised that their leader had entered the conversation at all. "Besides the occasional polar bear, the jaguar is the only beast who actually hunts humans. There are many other species who attack us—if they think we're endangering them—and there are many species of animals who eat the flesh of a corpse—but the jaguar seeks people out."

"For dinner? Great! All I need to hear after sitting next to this looney tune all the way from Miami." Nanos walked over to Billy Two and stood before him with a questioning face. "And what does it mean, tell me that? I'm going to be luncheon for two at the best restaurant in the Amazon or something?"

"It means that we should do nothing to anger the gods of the jungle," Billy Two said softly, but with great meaning. "It means that those gods will not let themselves be forgotten the way the Incas did. If someone tries to make it happen, then the jaguar will move through the night and he will be the means by which the gods fight back—with blood dripping from the fangs of the hunting cats."

Barrabas and Beck looked at each other and said nothing. But they each knew the other one had images of huge crop-dusting planes dropping their loads of herbicides over the Amazon jungle.

"THE WHOLE THING in Hollywood stinks so badly you can't believe it. Hell, those guys were the worst bunch of..."

"If you don't calm down, Liam, I'm going to have to start treating you for high blood pressure." Lee Hatton looked at the big Irishman across the table set up by room service in Nile's suite for their dinner. Her smile melted away the anger that O'Toole had been venting at the rest of the group over the meal.

"Well," he said, his voice much calmer, "it was a great disappointment. I tell you, it was the worst."

"It had to be, to have something you care about so very much tossed around so unthinkingly," Lee said. She reached out and put her hand over Liam's wrist. None of the other men who were watching the scene would have been able to do that. As close as they were, and as much as they understood the emotions of men in war, that sort of kind touch was something they weren't comfortable with.

But each and every one of them was happy that Lee was there and able to do it.

Liam O'Toole's attempt to have his poetry accepted and read in the world was a personal struggle of his that they had all been watching during their many years together as a team. The drive to get that recognition was one of Liam's great weaknesses, and had even gotten the team in trouble with an enemy that had known about it and used the vulnerability as a way to get to the SOBs.

None of the men was worried about that, though. They only wanted their friend and compatriot to be happy and achieve what he wanted to achieve. The Hollywood gig with the big star, Malcolm MacMalcolm, had been one of the most hopeful possibilities that Liam had come up with so far.

"We have a job to do." Nile stood from the table and threw his napkin down. The others got up without a single complaint. All of them, certainly including Liam, knew that Nile wasn't denying the importance of their conversation. They also knew that they were there for exactly the reason he'd just given them—to do a job.

The team gathered their chairs in a circle around Barrabas. They watched as he gathered his material together and prepared for their briefing.

The SOBs all arrived in La Paz on schedule, well trained, well conditioned and committed to their work. It was understood, though, that the direction the team took was even more important to Barrabas's life than it was to any of their own.

Through Jessup, "the Fixer"—and sometimes on his own—it was Nile who came up with their assignments. He gathered the group together and coordinated their campaigns. In return for unflinching loyalty and for their personal skills, the SOBs received a great deal of money, enough to have long since satisfied their desires for security and the luxury of their dreams.

Having the money never tempted any of them to leave the team. They no longer had to have the sums that were quietly deposited into their numbered accounts in a Swiss bank whenever their jobs were completed. That wasn't their motivation. Their motivation wasn't simplistically idealistic, either. They certainly weren't for hire to just anyone with the bucks to pay them, and they also weren't cowboys—out to save the whole world.

They were a team. There are certain things that happen to people who have been together many times in combat. Psychologists like to talk about the "bonding" that takes place. The experience of intense and total trust under fire and the knowledge that life depends on the surrounding teammates in the middle of a battle, makes it hard to be alone when it's over.

They could look around that room, and each could remember an occasion when he or she had been saved by one of the others. It's hard to go back after that, to go back to being just a person on the street in the midst of strangers, who don't understand what it is that makes you tick and what are the demons that cross your mind when you can't sleep at night. It's better to be together, with the team, with those people who understand.

When Nile was ready to begin, each one of them saw something familiar come over him. They looked up at Barrabas and realized that he had assumed the role of the "colonel," the rank he'd achieved in the United States Army during the Vietnam conflict. They saw a man in control, and a man who was as ready for action as he was used to it.

That was part of them all, as well. If the money wasn't their motivation, the adventure was. Each of them had tried sitting at home and being a regular person—living a normal life—and knew it wasn't for him or her. What was for them was the quest for excitement and the desire to achieve.

They could see themselves reflected back in the eyes of Nile Barrabas. They realized that he wasn't downplaying the danger involved in one of their missions, but they knew that something about him needed the challenges their missions constantly gave them. There was a response to that—to being in Bolivia, to the knowledge that there was such a thing as war and battle and that it might come down on them at any moment. Barrabas wasn't just willing to accept it, he wanted it, and deep in his soul, he needed it.

They waited impatiently for him to begin.

"This is a large country, bigger than Texas, with more variety to the kinds of climate and terrain inside its borders than just about any other in the world. From here, high in the Andes with peaks over 23,000 feet, to the jungles of the Chapare, from the waters of Titicaca to the near-deserts on the border with Argentina—there are incredible extremes to Bolivia's geography.

"Our matériel needs aren't clear yet because of that. Liam and Claude, I want you to do some scouting around here in

La Paz to see what you can find available for purchase locally. Don't hesitate to use the black market if you have to—I bet it's lively in a place like this, especially after the disruption of the recent revolt.

"We have to prepare for everything and anything. Alpine equipment if we need to go to the mountains, swamp boats if we need to go in the Chapare, all-terrain vehicles for the plains."

"You got it, Nile," Claude answered for the pair. O'Toole was still struggling to come back from his depression about his Hollywood experience, and he only nodded.

"Lee," Nile went on, "you're our best bet on chemistry."

"My med school labs were a long time ago," Lee warned.

"I trust them. Seems like most of your education's done pretty well by us so far," Barrabas answered. "We're looking at the possibility that a form of synthetic cocaine is being manufactured somewhere in Bolivia. I need you to get very nosy with import/export firms here and start to track some of the ways that chemicals might be getting into the country.

"One thing we know: there's probably a Swedish connection in all of this. I've explained that to each of you individually, but it's worth going over again quickly. Some kind of secret research being done by the Gustavus Adolphus Institute was discovered by the Swedish prime minister. That discovery probably got him killed. The head scientist of the institute—a man named Lennart Moberg—disappeared after the assassination. No one knows for sure why, or how. About the same time, just after the assassination, one of the prime minister's off-duty bodyguards also was missing. It's suspicious to say the least.

"Moberg is a wild card. We don't know if he's a victim or a conspirator. At this point, it doesn't much matter.

"Lee, it's a long shot, but wonder about Swedish-brand chemicals in particular. If there is someone here in Bolivia who does, in fact, have a formula for cocaine, it may be that the drug is being made from ordinary materials that wouldn't, by themselves, be paid attention to. But the odds are that the Swedish chemist would stick to ingredients he already knew about.

"We also know that Bolivian customs isn't really a factor—they're as crooked here as they come—so it isn't them that our quarry is hiding from.

"I bet that's an encouragement for being very sloppy. We just need to see if we can find some large shipments of apparently unnecessary chemicals that are probably Scandinavian in origin, and trace where they're being shipped to."

"But, Nile," Lee said, "we haven't a clue what chemicals they're using to make this stuff...if they are making it."

"I know," Nile admitted, "but we have to take these shots in the dark. Where they're really doing what is the question.

"Which brings me to you, Alex, and Billy Two."

The Greek looked up at the colonel. "Yeah," he said hopefully. He'd really been wishing that Barrabas would send him off on an assignment with someone other than the Osage, but it was a hope against hope. Among all the team members, Billy Two and Alex were the closest pair, or had been until the pressures and tensions of Hawk Spirit had started to get to them.

"I want you two to go undercover. My information says that you've a few...interesting contacts with some dealers in Florida."

"Me!" Nanos exclaimed. "I've only been partying with some dudes who know some hot ladies...."

"Your dudes happen to include José Suarez?" Nile asked.

"José's a bitchin' guy, Nile! I mean, the man knows how to throw a party!"

"He is one of the very worst of them. I'm glad this is out in the open, Nile," Billy Two said in his most judgmental voice. "You're right, Alex has been fraternizing with many people who insult the memories of the Carib gods."

Nile stood there in amazement and didn't quite understand what Billy Two had just said to him, but then decided he didn't want to know, anyway. It was one piece of intelligence he didn't have to have.

"José is a main man on the Florida Keys," Nanos growled as he glared across the room at Billy Two.

"Suarez is not a man," Billy Two scoffed. "He's a golf player who drinks too much."

"Wait a minute! Hold on!" Nile threw up his hands to stop the verbal exchange before it went any further. "My own intelligence says you're both right. Suarez is a golfer—he's got a great handicap by all reports, in fact—and he is the biggest party giver in South Florida. There is a reason for all those parties, Alex. José Suarez is the biggest dealer in South Florida.

"Forget your fighting and realize that I don't give a damn what he is socially, religiously or criminally. The only important thing about José Suarez now is that he's a recognized name in the international drug trade. And Nanos knows him, and Suarez would probably vouch for him if there was a phone call made to verify Alex's identity. You're going to use him, Alex.

"He's your in. You're going to start infiltrating the kind of circles here in Bolivia where you can make a connection with someone who can sell you a whopping amount of cocaine. It'll give you another chance to see where their delivery could be made from.

"Nate, I need a major communication center with highly transportable gear set up, right here in this suite. Will it work?"

"Sure, Nile. The height of the building is just great for that, especially with the terrace. I'll check and see if we can't move up to the twenty-fifth floor, just for an added boost. The mountains might pose a difficulty, but I can work with that, find a way around them."

"Good, get cracking on it.

"Geoff, you and I are going to do some work with the Bolivian military. They're supposed to be corrupted beyond belief, but I know there have to be some good men here.

"There was a contingent of Bolivians in Nam—just a token force, but they were damned good. We're going to look some of them up and hope they can give us a hand."

"My pleasure, boss."

"Everyone: We're looking for a cache of cocaine big enough to ruin the mucous membranes of half the citizens of the United States. We're also looking for a factory under construction that can produce cocaine in some manner other than from the coca plant, one we don't even know about.

"We have a big job to do. Let's go do it."

8

"Billy Two, listen to me." Alex Nanos watched as the big Osage sat closed-eyed and cross-legged on the floor of their room at the International. "You have to get dressed and you have to dress as though you look real."

The last comment finally got Billy Two to open his eyes. "If I'm not dressed *real*, I don't know what real is."

"What you are is dressed like a savage Osage on the Great Plains. This, however, is Bolivia where you have to dress like the sidekick to an international drug dealer. Get it?"

"Hrmph!" Billy Two muttered, but he did stand up. He was dressed in nothing but the traditional loin cloth of his people. The flaps of naturally cured leather only barely covered the crotch and left most of his butt hanging out nude. He had a bone armor plate over his chest, and the omnipresent Seminole amulet hung from his neck.

"The job must be done, I suppose," Billy Two said. "I need to prove to you that I'm not what you called me—a 'looney tune.' So I will. I'll dress like your gangster friends in Florida, and we'll go off and do the job right."

"Thank you, O noble savage," Alex said disgustedly. "You're doing me such a great favor and honor by submitting to the needs of this enterprise." Nanos's voice dripped with sarcasm, but Billy Two ignored it as he stripped. He'd actually only been wearing the outfit for his meditations, and as that activity was proving extremely difficult in a modern hotel room, he'd decided to give up.

The truth was seeping out in a sly smile that was curling the ends of Billy Two's mouth as he stepped into his shorts. He got a white T-shirt out of his bags and dragged it over his large, muscular chest.

There was no question in Billy Two's mind that he'd had a major mystical experience. The trip to the South Pacific that he'd made with the rest of the team on their last assignment had changed him completely. He'd gone into it with a desperate desire to find out if his god—Hawk Spirit—existed. It did. He'd been saved by it, he'd talked to it, and he'd revered it. No one and no thing was ever going to be able to convince him otherwise.

But, as Billy Two next pulled on his dress slacks, he also realized that the idea of Hawk Spirit was something with which he could really have fun with his pal, Nanos. Like all truly religious people, Billy Two didn't have a need to talk about his god all the time. What was important was that he knew the truth of it. He wanted times like the past few hours he'd spend in meditation, and he wanted to know that he was in harmony with Hawk Spirit as he led his life, and that Hawk Spirit was going to be beside him when he went to battle. But he probably wouldn't have mentioned the existence of the god or his own personal relationship with him to Alex Nanos so often if it hadn't been so much fun.

Hawk Spirit made Alex crazy. And Billy Two intended to make sure the god continued to do that for a long time.

As Billy Two buttoned his shirt, he turned around and saw that Alex was waiting, already dressed, wearing a suit that was just a shade too loud, a bit too flashy, an inch too fashionable for the Greek's big, powerful torso.

The outfit made Nanos look like a hood, which was just the image he wanted. Billy Two caught sight of himself in

the mirror and saw a man who was just too regular looking. If they were going to go out there and act as though they
were both criminals, something had to be done about the
too tasteful appearance. The hair! he thought with inspira-
tion.

"Just a sec, Alex," Billy Two said as he grabbed a traveling kit and went into the bathroom. Alex hadn't noticed
that the Osage had taken Nanos's kit; they used similar plain
black leather outfits.

"Probably putting on war paint," Nanos sputtered under his breath.

But when Billy Two came back out, it wasn't paint that
had altered his looks. "Think this passes the white man's
test for sleaze?" the Osage asked.

"Blast, but I wouldn't want to meet you in a dark alley,"
Alex answered with honest awe.

Billy Two had taken some of the oil Nanos sometimes
used on his own hair, and he'd applied it to his thick and
heavy mane. Billy Two's hair no longer hung free and loose
about his neck, instead it was slicked back in imitation of a
gangster on the make in Little Italy in the 1930s. The waves
of greased hair seemed to give the Osage an air of danger
and intrigue.

Billy Two's skin was olive colored, and he didn't look
Italian at all, but the mellowed tanned complexion seemed
to become part of the same picture as the hair. It was just the
way the locks were swept backward on the side and then together and sort of up in a duck's ass that made the image.
The huge slick pompadour on the top of his head supplied
the final emphasis. It seemed to add a full two inches to Billy
Two's already substantial height.

"And for the final touch!" Billy Two went to the garment bag hanging in the closet and pulled out a white tux-
edo jacket. In other times, that very suit would have gotten

him into the most exclusive casinos and clubs in the world. That was why he'd brought it. That kind of cover was much more common in the SOBs' activities than the current gangsterlike appearance. But at the moment, the effect of the garment over the dark dress slacks he had on rather than the formal pants he usually wore with it was still slightly sinister.

Billy Two had just transformed himself from a near-naked aborigine into a modern-day hood in a matter of minutes.

"Nah," Alex said as he studied his friend with new-found appreciation. "That's not the final touch—this is going to be." He went to his own bag and dragged out a heavy .357 Magnum, along with a shoulder holster. "Put this on."

"Alex, that cannon's going to be obvious to anyone. It's going to be a huge bulge underneath this light jacket."

"That's the whole point, Billy boy. You are going to be the most evil-looking, hard-assed gunner in this city. When we start to move through the darkness of La Paz, they're all going to see you coming for miles.

"They will want to find out just who you are and why you're by my side. You're bait, Billy Two. You're all the proof I'm ever going to need that I'm a real gangster."

"Let's get into it, Alex. Let's really get into this one and enjoy ourselves."

"We're off to the races, dude, and we got the fastest horse on the track all of a sudden."

IT'S NOT DIFFICULT to find the centers of crime in any city, no matter what its size or what continent it's on. The local newspapers provide the first step. In their advertisements for night spots, there are notices for a very few, very expensive, very flashy clubs.

Billy Two and Alex Nanos had their act down perfectly by the time they got to the Club Carnivale in La Paz. The place wasn't as loud and raucous as usual; the "revolution" had scared away planeloads of tourists from North America and Europe. It made the two of them all the more welcome.

The act the two had perfected was simple for them to carry out; it fit their personalities very well. Nanos was up front, the big man with the quick smile at the women and the easy handshake and big bucks for the waiters. He grotesquely overtipped the maître d', just to start things off right. The word spread that the American was good for a lot of money, and it got him plenty of attention.

Billy Two was the icing on the cake. His weapon pressed against his suit jacket so that only a fool couldn't see it, and even a bigger fool wouldn't have been able to figure out what caused it. He carefully walked one step behind Nanos. He was the bodyguard, looking around just as carefully as the Greek, but not at the women or the potential friends. Billy Two was looking hard, unsmiling, to see if there was any danger at the club.

Even when they sat down, Billy Two seemed to sit farther back from the table than Nanos did, almost as though he weren't one of the party, but an observer, someone who didn't expect to take part in the happenings.

It really was the hair that did it. The scantily clad women who wove their way through the tables on the main floor of the Club Carnivale stared at it, as though it was a totem of masculinity. Styles come and go, but the recent wave of French crime movies and some of the American films that fed on nostalgia for the 1930s had made the greased-back, long-haired look a universal symbol of danger and malice.

"Billy Two, you are one mean-looking dude right now," Nanos said to his partner while he continued to flash his big pearly whites at the seminude dancers on the stage. "I didn't know you had it in you."

Just for good measure, and to keep Nanos on his toes, Billy Two replied, "Hawk Spirit won't like it."

"To hell with him," Nanos answered. He wasn't even going to rise to that invitation to a fight. "Looks like we have some company coming," he said to change the subject.

Ernesto Revo was the owner of the club. He knew how to work the business for all it was worth, and he knew who else's business he needed to feed if he wanted to stay alive. The whole idea was to have a club that was just what his represented: a big, colorful tourist trap that would lure a lot of people. Ernesto knew he would end up sending some of his customers on to other places. His recommendations would make certain people who were very important very happy.

The two Americans would be welcome in certain spots in town, and Ernesto would be happy to get them there. He only had to figure out just what place they might find the most compatible—and he had to get rid of the gun, he added the afterthought to himself.

"Señores!" He smiled at the one who was obviously in charge. He also tried to avoid looking at the face of the other one, the one with the piece of metal against his chest, whose face was devoid of any emotion.

Ernesto snapped a finger and a waitress was by his side immediately. "You'll have one of our famous Titicaca Rum Volcanoes, won't you. It is, of course, on the house."

The waitress didn't wait for the two guests to answer, but ran to fill Ernesto's order at once.

"Now, gentlemen, what can we do for you here at the Club Carnivale? The food is excellent—I eat it myself—but there must be special entertainments you gentlemen would like."

Ernesto leaned forward to hear their answer just as a loud band began to play brassy Spanish music from the podium. "The girls will finish dancing soon, and I will happily introduce you to any one of them whom you think you might enjoy. Or perhaps you would prefer a personal recommendation to Madame L'España's. It is the finest house of 'recreation' in La Paz."

Neither Alex nor Billy Two so much as blinked.

"You'd prefer boys?" Ernesto turned to survey the band members. "The trumpet player, him I could get you."

When Ernesto turned back to the Americans, he could see that there was still no response. Something else much more comforting to him, also became apparent. His two chief bouncers had caught the action and had obviously been told about the pistol-packing American. They now stood behind Billy Two, one on either side of him.

"Whatever you'd enjoy, gentlemen, I'm afraid the fact that you are armed will upset my other customers. I must ask for your gun."

Ernesto held out his palm, feeling confident with his enforcers so close by. Billy Two looked at the outstretched hand as though it was some kind of alien bug. Then he looked up at Ernesto with that same expression of wonderment.

"Nah," Nanos answered, but Ernesto didn't have time to continue the conversation. Billy Two decided to take things on his own course. He stood up, slowly and casually, as though he might even be reaching into his jacket to get the requested gun, after all. When he was halfway up, his elbows shot back with all the speed possible by the human body. The two goons were caught by Billy Two's arms, and they both collapsed forward, the breath knocked out of them.

Billy Two lifted up his arms again, and on the next round, his elbows delivered blows to the bouncers' necks, knocking them out cold. Then the Osage calmly sat down. He still didn't smile.

"Where are the people who make this town work?" Nanos demanded in a low, even voice.

Ernesto studied his open palm with shock, and he seemed to be glad it was still there. He couldn't find his voice, though. He only stared at the hand.

The waitress returned with their drinks at that moment. She'd missed the action and, since her boss wasn't saying anything about it, she thought it was a good idea to ignore the two unconscious bodies on the floor by the table.

The Carnivale's special Titicaca Rum Volcanoes were placed on the table in front of Nanos and Billy Two.

"Firewater, no good," Billy Two said and pushed the drink away, purposely spilling it over Ernesto's hand.

That brought the club manager to life. "Who are you?" he asked in a strangled voice. "What trouble do you want to give me?" Ernesto was making quick nervous movements, rubbing the residue of the sweet, sticky rum drink off himself using the tablecloth to try to sponge up the rest of it.

Ernesto was honestly alarmed. People like him were dependent on others for protection, real protection in the sense of influence. Bouncers might be able to handle a few rambunctious tourists, but the reality was that Bolivia was a lawless land. With Martinez gone, the gangs who ruled the underworld of the country were having a field day. The one thing that might have kept them in check had disappeared.

Who were the new powers that were going to evolve, and who was going to end up on top of the heap? Ernesto was desperately trying to figure that out. He didn't have an answer yet, not one he could trust. The appearance of truly dangerous men in his club terrified him.

"No trouble, sport," Nanos said quietly. "I just asked you an easy question. Where's the people who really run this town?"

Ernesto looked up at him again and made some fast, silent calculations. One of them had the same result every time he figured it: get these two out of his place. No cops—as if that would ever do any good in Bolivia—and no more tries to outdo them. Just make them be gone.

"There's a place on the other side of the Plaza de la République. Maria's. There are many people there. She'll introduce you to all of them. My men—other men—they'll take you there in my car. Right now."

"YOU REALLY DID THAT to poor Ernesto?" the woman called Maria asked Alex a short while later.

"He did." Nanos jerked his thumb toward Billy Two who was standing in his hood's costume up against the wall of the dive. Maria's place was much less ostentatious than the Club Carnivale, but there was an air of authenticity to it that the Greek knew would have made it a hit if it ever got in the tour guides.

The singer who was performing with a single guitar was telling tales so sad Alex didn't even have to understand the language to know how sorry about life that woman was. The tears came out with every phrase; the hurt spread with every chorus.

There was a full bar, but most of the patrons weren't interested in fancy mixed drinks or even in the social class of top-shelf Scotch. They were drinking from unimpressive bottles of red wine. Alex and Maria were sharing one that stood on the table between them. The wine was new and tasted sharp, but it was good. It was doing the trick for them, that was for sure.

Maria studied Billy Two. "Him? If you weren't so interesting, I'd tumble him. Looks good. Big muscles. Big hands, too. You know what they say about big hands?"

Nanos didn't answer but drank in the sight of Maria. She was gorgeous in the most earthy of earthy ways. Though she wasn't as young as she'd been once, Alex didn't care. She wasn't over any hill he wouldn't climb. Dark mascara emphasized her dark eyes, and the lipstick she was wearing was blood-red.

Her black dress clung to her like a glove, and it was obviously meant to. If Maria had ever been a shy or coy young lady, the phase had passed so quickly she probably couldn't remember it herself.

Maria was hard. Another woman, one who was striving herself for some kind of respectability, would have called her cheap. Some men would have called her a slut just by looking at her. Nanos called her dynamite.

"So, what do you want that's so bad you got to rough up Ernesto's place, huh?" Maria took a hit of her wine after she asked the question and stared directly at Nanos.

"Got some friends in Florida—the Keys—who have been hearing some stuff about Bolivia and the availability of some very controlled substances that, even if they weren't controlled, wouldn't be very legal. Seems they just wanted some things checked out down here. It was worth the airfare."

"You going to play that game with me? Not tell me more?" Maria was disgusted with the way Nanos was starting the whole thing.

"José Suarez, he's this friend of mine. Seems it should be likely that the sound of his voice would make a lot of people interested in talking to me."

Maria lighted a cigarette from the candle burning on the table. She used the smoke that curled up over her face as an excuse to narrow her eyes at Nanos, camouflaging the intensity with which she was studying him.

"A name?" She shrugged. "I can send out some word with that. And anything else?"

"A numbered bank account in Switzerland that's big enough to convince you to forget your mother's name."

"I never knew it," Maria said without emotion. "I don't think it would impress me that much, either.

"Tell you what." She stood from the table and her smoothly rounded belly was now right in front of him. "I'll send out some word about your money and your friend. It'll take some time. You want to waste it here? Listen to the canary sing—" she nodded to the performer singing another tangolike dirge "—or you want to come up to my apartment, see if we can't find a better way to pass the time?"

"What about my pal?"

"You want him to come, too?" Maria looked at Billy Two with lustful speculation. "Yeah, we could do that."

"No, no, that's not what I meant. What's he going to do while you and I are . . . passing the time?"

Billy Two was surveying the whole scene without a single evidence of emotion. His eyes were the only part of him that moved as they followed the conversation between the other two.

"If he stands here like that for a single minute after I leave, every one of the girls who work for me will be hitting up on him." Maria's eyes swept up and down Billy Two's strong physique. It was only the promise of Nanos having more lasting power—the thing that Maria liked most in a man—that kept her from changing her mind about who her companion ought to be.

"He'll be okay." She looked back at the Greek. "Unless you think you need him for protection."

"Oh, no, lady," he said, standing up, "I don't want protection from anything you got for me."

"Let's go. I'll talk to my bartender on the way upstairs, and he'll start it all, get some people interested in what you're up to so they'll come looking for you."

Maria began to lead Nanos away. She threw Billy Two one last look that ended with a smile he understood perfectly well. It meant *"Sometime soon, man, sometime real soon."*

BILLY TWO WAS SPRAWLED OUT on the floor of Maria's second floor apartment corridor, right outside her bedroom. His suit jacket was rolled up under his head and served as a pillow. He ignored the sounds of flesh pounding against flesh and sweat sucking on sweat that came from under the door.

Nanos's sex life wasn't capturing his interest just then. If the Greek wanted to put it to a woman from whom he might be able to get some good information, that was fine with him.

What was more important to Billy Two was himself and Hawk Spirit. Things were getting very interesting.

He felt he had achieved control of the god. He was very much at peace with himself, in a way he had never been before. The exercises he went through to contact Hawk Spirit—his meditations—gave him a sense of incredible well-being. Before, Hawk Spirit had come and gone at his own pace, when he wanted to.

But now Billy Two was realizing that he could conjure Hawk Spirit when he needed him, and that he could also keep it from appearing when him was a distraction.

The reason the others thought he was insane, Billy Two understood with sudden insight, was that Hawk Spirit used to arrive in his brain unbeckoned. They couldn't see the reason for his being there.

That new chapter, giving Billy Two power over Hawk Spirit's appearances, had begun high in the Sierras in California months ago, when he'd performed the ceremonies of his ancestors. Hawk Spirit had come to him then, when he'd asked him to, and had stayed with him when he'd been in trouble in the Pacific.

Then, when Billy Two had gone on vacation with Nanos, the god had retreated, only appearing when Billy Two had requested his help.

To be able to call your own god when you wanted him! And then to be a normal human being when you wanted to be on your own! That was deep shit, that was wonderful deep shit, Billy Two thought with a big smile on his face.

A new sound interrupted his thoughts, and it had nothing to do with Nanos and the lady jumping on each other's bones on the other side of the door. The noises were of booted feet climbing stairs, very slowly, trying unsuccessfully to move silently.

Billy Two reached into his holster and brought out the Magnum. The god wasn't necessary for a minor human encounter, the Indian thought to himself. He'd just trust his cannon for the job at hand.

He crawled down the corridor on his elbows and knees and leaned out to look down into the stairwell. It harbored three uniformed men, each one carrying an American-made M-16. Their insignia showed members of the Bolivian armed forces. If they hadn't worked so hard to be sneaky, Billy Two might have thought they were safe.

But anyone who was trying that hard to reach the upper floor of Maria's without detection had to be up to no good.

Billy Two put the big Magnum between his hands to steady it, knowing that the gun would have a kick to it like a bronco if he ever fired it.

Should he? Or should he wait for some other indication of what the Bolivians were up to?

In the next moment the leader of the trio gave Billy Two his answer. He handed his M-16 to the second man and used his now-free hands to reach into a belt sheath and retrieve a heavy, sharp-looking knife. The Osage deduced that no one was coming up those stairs armed like that unless he was up to something that wasn't going to be stopped by easy negotiations.

Billy Two jumped to his feet, spread his legs in a firing stance and aimed straight downward. "Freeze!" he shouted. Even if the men didn't understand English, they would understand that universal sound.

The two men who still had M-16s did just as they were told. They looked up at the hoodlum with the slicked-back hair and didn't move a muscle. Their leader was the one who was going to be the hero. He must have thought he was really something special. He didn't have a rifle anymore, but he did have that knife.

Moving quickly, so quickly that even Billy Two barely understood what he was doing, he grabbed the blade of his knife and dropped the weapon down underarm. He brought it up in a blazing-fast motion, launching the tool in a quick upward arc, aiming the deadly steel right at Billy Two.

The Osage's body responded before his mind did. He jerked backward and heard the knife whistle past his cheek, missing him by a combination of seconds and fractions of an inch to hit the ceiling. Still acting on pure reflex, Billy Two had pulled the trigger, and the powerful handgun had blasted away. Its huge bullets slammed into the Bolivian's skull, shattering it and sending a spray of blood against the hallway walls even before the man's body had time to hit the floor.

The reverberations of the explosions echoed through the closed space of the stairwell. The other two men had jumped at the sound of the Magnum's rounds, but then they had frozen to the spot, their faces showing greater awe for the fearsome-looking American gangster.

Maria's bedroom door flew open. A very naked and very excited Alex Nanos jumped out, his hands in a fighting stance, ready to try to help if he was needed.

"Get your skirt, Nanos," Billy Two said calmly. "We need her to ask these two jokers some questions."

The Greek's hands dropped down, and he made a vain attempt to cover himself. "Jesus, Billy Two, couldn't you have waited just one more minute? I mean, I was . . ."

"Get her," Billy Two said slowly and carefully. "We got more important things to talk to her about than that."

"It was that damned Hawk Spirit of yours again," Nanos muttered as he turned to do his pal's bidding.

Billy Two didn't move an eyelid as he kept the two silent and quivering Bolivians in his sight. But the very same thought had crossed his own mind as he tried to reconstruct the speed of his reaction to the danger. Maybe it had been Hawk Spirit again.

9

Maria sat on her bed filing her fingernails. She was wearing only an old red satin robe that kept falling open as she moved, giving the four men in the room occasional flashes of flesh. Only Alex Nanos seemed to care. Billy Two was oblivious, and the two Bolivian soldiers were so concerned about the Osage that they weren't about to notice any woman, no matter how lewdly she showed off her bare skin. They had watched their leader's dead body being carried off by two of Maria's bartenders. That was a much more pressing reality for them. They wanted to make sure they didn't take the same free ride.

Their prospects weren't so hot. Billy Two had taken their belts and, along with some other items from Maria's bureaus, used them to truss them up as tightly as turkeys ready for the oven. The two soldiers were each securely bound to a hard-backed chair. The ferocious-looking Osage was standing in front of them, and they were waiting for him to make his next move. What that was going to be was foremost in the minds of the two Bolivians, and it was obvious from the way they stared at the hulking American Indian.

"Well, I'm not going to say I loved you too much to turn you in," Maria said to Nanos without looking up from her task. "That'd be bullshit. I guess there's no reason for you to believe that I didn't have anything to do with these jokers. I did what you wanted me to do: I put out the word that there were some North Americans nosing around who were making a lot of noise about money and cocaine. They responded.'' She shrugged. ''It's what you said you wanted them to do. They just didn't do it the exact way you hoped.

''Trust? In me? Why should you?'' Now Maria did look up from her work with the emery board. ''I'll tell you why: if you make a connection, I get a commission. You get killed? I get nothing.

''I'm a businesswoman, pure and simple. I don't throw away profits like that.''

Nanos took an apple from a fruit bowl on Maria's dresser and bit into it furiously. He was fighting against a fury of conflicting emotions that were battling inside him. His fast chewing and the loud crack of the crisp apple gave sound effects to his thoughts.

Besides the usual tension experienced during a mission, he felt sexually frustrated, which further complicated things. Those passing visions of her body reminded him painfully of the interruption in their evening. Distrust flooded through him, as well, though her point seemed probably correct. But concern was also part of his feelings. Why had they attracted that kind of attention?

''Ask them why they came after me,'' Billy Two suddenly said to Maria, ending her conversation with the Greek.

She shot a volley of questions at the two prisoners in Spanish. The first man who answered her spoke with a defiant tone. Billy Two didn't need a translation to know that the man was going to try to be a hero.

The Osage was smiling even before he listened to Maria's translation. He had retrieved for a trophy the knife that had been thrown at him. He pulled it out of his belt now and used it to pare his nails. It was a strange and violent image after the petite emery board that Maria had been using on her own nails.

"Tell him," Billy Two said without looking at Maria, "that I'm going to use this knife to slit open his pants."

"You gonna get kinky on him?" Maria asked teasingly.

Billy Two shot her a hard look, and Maria gave up her joke. She shot the words to the captive. He answered, but tried to sit up straighter in his chair, straining against his bonds to regain some dignity.

"Then," Billy Two continued to speak as he picked up one of the apples from the fruit bowl, "I'm going to cut off just one of his balls." Billy Two threw the apple into the air. It bounced off the ceiling and hurtled back down. When it did, Billy Two's knife was waiting. The sharp steel blade sliced the apple, sending two almost perfectly equal halves to the floor.

Maria spoke in Spanish while she and the two captives took in Billy Two's knife act.

"And I'm going to feed him that one ball," Billy Two said, "and make him swallow it." Billy Two dramatically stepped on one of the apple halves and crushed it with the heel of his boot. Maria was speaking quickly to keep up with Billy Two's commentary. "Then we'll go for the other one."

The man finally spoke to Maria in a hushed whisper, and she translated. "He thinks you're sick," Maria said. "He thinks you're a barbarian."

"Always have been, always will be," Billy Two said emotionlessly. "Tell him to talk now, or else he'll find out just what kind of tribe my people come from."

Maria's Spanish seemed to be slower now, as though she had decided to take Billy Two more seriously and was trying, just with her manner of talking, to communicate to the soldiers that they had better do likewise.

Billy Two's raw psychological technique worked. Both men began to talk at once as they looked at the squashed apple half and realized the same could happen to a part of their own bodies. The man would have treated them with as few feelings as he'd shown for the fruit.

"They were sent here because they were told that you were North American drug dealers," Maria continued. "Their officers have orders to rid the country of your type." Astonished by that statement, Maria backtracked in her own quick Spanish to cross-examine the soldier even before Billy Two could ask her to.

"He says that the word is out—among the police, the National Guard—that the drug trade is to be consolidated." Maria screwed up her brow in an uncustomary frown. "They say the new regime has decreed that everything will end on the streets of La Paz—all the drug dealing, all the drug trade. The coca that is passed around will only be the rough, undistilled form that the Bolivian people have used for generations. The fine powder that makes so much money in North America is forbidden."

Maria paused and turned to Billy Two, so shocked that she had to wait before she could voice her disbelief. "Bolivia is really going to go straight? It can't be. But this new regime has been in power for only a week or so.... Could it actually be trying to do this?

"If it did—" Maria looked away, her mind churning with possibilities "—there'd be an uprising among the criminals. But so far the big-time guys are still happy. They're the ones with the regular connections with North America, the ones who've made real fortunes off the dope. The small-timers, the middle men, they can always go elsewhere. They don't have enough power to make problems.

"This Valdez, the new one in the presidential palace, he's got something very strange going on if he's pulling this off, friends. You better forget your drugs and your drug dealing. If Valdez is moving in this direction, taking over the control of the supply and using only the biggest of the exporters, then he's going to be a very powerful president, after all."

"CLAUDE, YOU'RE CRAZY," Liam O'Toole said once again as he and his friend were rushing down the main avenues of La Paz in a taxicab.

The big black man just smiled behind his designer sunglasses. "I think it's a stroke of genius. Not only do we get absolutely everything we need, we also give you a way to get back at those assholes in Hollywood. This is the most wonderful revenge on an entire industry I've ever heard of."

O'Toole just shook his head and looked down at himself once more. Those were his clothes?

Claude had insisted that the two of them go to the most expensive and most fashionable men's store in La Paz. There, he'd bought them outfits of extraordinary expense and questionable taste. Their slacks were pleated, their jackets were raw silk, their shoes were made of paper-thin Italian glove leather, and their ties had some unknown person's initials embossed on them. They were movie moguls. There was no doubt about it. The two-hundred-dollar sunglasses were the final touch.

Hollywood had come to Bolivia!

"There is one thing that every red-blooded person in the free world respects," Claude intoned, "and that's movies. There is one thing in the world that almost everyone wants to have something to do with, and that's movies.

"Do you realize that the Yugoslavs provided twenty-five thousand soldiers free of charge to be extras in a Bible epic? Do you realize that Spain destroyed half its wheat crop once for a tired remake of *El Cid*? Most people will do anything to have something to do with moviemaking.

"The Bolivian army is going to be in the palm of our hands. You just wait and see. And while it's happening, you are going to lay the groundwork for some very difficult times for Mr. Malcolm MacMalcolm."

Just then the cab pulled in front of the administrative offices of the National Guard. Hayes, enjoying his charade, handed the driver a big tip and then, using his knowledge of Spanish, asked him to wait for them. The cabbie—part of a breed that doesn't change from city to city or country to country—stared at the big bills the American had put into his hands with awe, and finally conjured up a big smile while he assured the gentlemen that he would, in fact, wait for as long as they wanted him to.

Claude strode up the stairs of the grandly constructed building, past its statues commemorating long-forgotten battles and no-longer-recognized heroes. Red-haired Liam followed meekly by his side, at least as meekly as anyone his size and stature could.

Claude Hayes and Liam O'Toole were both massively muscular men who were well over six feet and would have stood out in any crowd, certainly they did in Bolivia. Their dramatic appearance was working in their favor, making them look bigger than life, more than mere mortals. They looked like producers for the silver screen.

As soon as they got through the front door of the building, Hayes was pounding on the reception desk. "I want to talk to the man in charge. I have a movie to make."

The word *movie* performed all the magic on the sergeant at the desk that Claude had promised. "Sir, who? What man in charge?"

"Who handles liaison with filmmakers?" Hayes demanded. "I have a project coming up that will star Malcolm MacMalcolm. An epic! It will be one of the great films of our history! I need an army!''

"An army?" the sergeant asked, unable to grasp what the American was saying. But there was one thing he did understand. His disbelief over Haye's request disintegrated as a smile of wonder came over his face. "Malcolm Mac-Malcolm!" he repeated with awe.

"Get me the moviemaking liaison!" Claude demanded, haughtily refusing to speak to the underling anymore.

While the man hurriedly began to phone various offices and speak to whoever was answering, Claude explained to O'Toole in a whisper, "Bolivia gets everything years later than the States. Your buddy MacMalcolm is still a star here. Their reruns are older than the Greek gods, and so he still looks young and fit."

O'Toole's expression tried to convey that he now doubted that the charlatan actor/producer could ever have been talented and been anything more than the going-to-fat waste of a man he'd just recently seen on the set in L.A.

"*Señores*, I'll take you to the third floor. General Estaban will see you himself!"

They hadn't a clue who Estaban was, but the way the receptionist spoke the name let them know they were going to the top for their next chapter.

"Hell, the power of those fools in Hollywood!" Liam sneered as they went toward the elevator.

"Ain't it grand?" Claude laughed back at him.

GENERAL RICARDO ESTABAN was the oldest member of the Bolivian military hierarchy. He'd survived countless revolutions and changes in administrations because he had learned never to take sides in any issue.

No matter what the regime, its leaders had understood that they needed someone like Estaban. He was the grand old man of the military. Now in his seventies, he looked great on horseback for parades, took a wonderful photograph and promptly saluted whoever held the key to the presidential palace, even if that key was still warm from someone else's blood.

Estaban wasn't anyone that the warring factions ever had to concern themselves with. He was, instead, a fixture, something one regime passed on to the next, leaving him free of any political encumberments.

Estaban had received every honor a living citizen and officer of Bolivia could get. He had even laid the foundation for those recognitions that could only come after a man had died. He had personally designed the postage stamp that would honor him when he passed over to the next world and had approved the memorial statue of himself scheduled to become the latest landmark of La Paz.

But General Ricardo Estaban had never been in a moving picture. And that was something he was going to have to do while he was still alive.

"Señores!" the general boomed in his theatrical baritone as soon as the two men from Hollywood entered his office. "It is such a pleasure for us to be honored with this visit."

The voice was the one that wowed them on Bolivian radio. The content of his broadcast messages was always meaningless, but the sound of them, his soothing tones, brought comfort to the masses, lulling children to sleep and giving adults a false sense of security. If they had a country with such a man high up in the military, certainly things couldn't be so very bad, could they? Estaban's touch with the media was one of many reasons his various superiors had kept him around—that, along with his willingness never to write his own material but rather to read whatever was put in front of him. He was a great communicator.

"Not a pleasure trip, General," Hayes said as he assumed the role of movie executive. He was fast-talking and rough around the edges. "We got a motion picture to get on with. Now, Mr. MacMalcolm—"

"Malcolm MacMalcolm?" Estaban asked with almost religious awe.

"The one and only," Hayes announced. "He'll star in this epic."

"Epic?" Estaban's excitement was turning him into a parroting dummy.

"Yeah, you know, the horses, the soldiers, the cast of thousands, all of it. We have a list of the help that we expect this country to cooperate with. After all, it's going to be quite a little catch for you guys to have the epic filmed here. You work for us because the conditions are right.

"We have a list of our requirements." Claude pulled a sheet of paper from his jacket's inside pocket and handed it to Estaban. "Just a few props that we'll need from your folks."

Estaban grabbed the paper quickly and read down the list. "Tanks? Helicopters? All-terrain vehicles? Gentlemen, a country with our limited resources—"

"No cooperation!" Claude said, his voice loaded with disgusted disbelief. "Don't you know what a public relations victory this would be for Bolivia? Don't you know the press you're going to get—which, if you don't mind my saying so, you could use after all that coke business that's been in the papers lately."

"But, gentlemen, this is such an extraordinary request!"

O'Toole knew it was his turn to cut in. He would have been hesitant about his ability to pull it off if he hadn't seen so recently the inanity that passed for acting on the set of an actual movie. "Hey, Claude!" he said, suddenly moving back and holding up his hands as though he were framing

Estaban in the viewfinder of an imaginary camera. "You know that one part we haven't cast yet? The one for the general who saves his country's honor?"

"Don't mention that to me!" Claude said as he grabbed to get the paper back. "We're going to Paraguay, where they know how to do things right, none of this bull..."

"No, no! Claude, look at this man! This is our costar."

"Costar?" Estaban said with renewed wonder.

"Not in Paraguay, he's not," Claude said, beginning to leave the office.

"Now, now, let's not be hasty!" Estaban said. He ran around his desk to block Hayes's exit. "For a man of Mr. MacMalcolm's integrity and for the honor of Bolivia, we can surely work out something agreeable."

Claude put the paper back into his pocket and tried to move around Estaban.

"Please!" The old general was begging now. "I'm sure we can do everything you ask of us."

"We can use him, Claude," O'Toole said, maintaining his role perfectly. "This man can stand in front of our cameras any day of the year."

Estaban had never been faced with such a torturous situation before in his life. He had been presented with a chance to be in a Hollywood film, a dream of a chance that was being fed by one of the North Americans, while the other didn't even let him have the paper that could lead to winning his place in the film world.

"Please!" the old man said one more time.

"We'll try it," Hayes said, his scowling face showing a definite lack of enthusiasm. Then he not only handed the general the paper, but also reached into his jacket again to retrieve even more sheets. "Here are the locations and the times we have to have the material."

"And me?" Estaban said weakly, hopefully.

"We're only doing the exteriors right now: the crowd scenes have to be in the can before MacMalcolm comes to La Paz in three more weeks."

"MacMalcolm will be here then?"

"That's how it's done," Liam said, trying to keep a straight face. "We can't have a man whose time is worth as much as his standing around while we move big machinery. We do all of that, and then we know precisely where to put him and the other stars for their lines later on. Like you. That's when we'll test you."

Other stars...like you... Ricardo Estaban had never heard such beautiful words before in his life.

"Yes, yes, of course, that's the way it is done." Estaban looked over the papers and realized that it would take a major mobilization of much of the Bolivian military to meet the list of demands. But the coup had succeeded, and there was nothing else planned.

Estaban's face took on a coy expression when he turned and saw his own reflection in the large mirror on the opposite wall. That profile had been deemed "perfect" by the post office artists. He saw the dignified way his skin had aged, which added still another level of character to his features. Was anything in his appearance less than perfect for the cinema? No! he answered his own question.

"It will be done this way!" Estaban said.

The rest of the conversation was lost on the old man. He had a secretary take notes on some of the other requirements the two North Americans had, knowing full well that he couldn't have retained the details himself. He was too busy imagining the premier of his movie debut.

10

Barrabas looked out over Lake Titicaca. It was beautiful, a body of deeply blue water, clean and remarkably untouched by civilization. La Paz was many miles away from the small fishing village where the shacks and the boats were all painted with bright primitive colors.

It was a part of Bolivia that tourists would seldom see, and the international press would never write about. The villagers were like so many other people in the world, simply folk who were only trying to make their way in the world and for whom the changes in government and the fate of international drug traffic were both alien thoughts.

The fish of the freshwater lake were the food that supplied them with much better diets than most poor people would ever have. High in protein and plentiful, the life that was taken from the lake was sustenance that kept the fishing people from suffering the grinding poverty of the mining regions. Nature was a generous provider at Titicaca, and life was good.

"I found the family's house, Colonel," Geoff Bishop reported as he came running up to the SOBs' leader. "Negara's family lives over there, in the one that's painted blue."

Barrabas looked at the small shack and tried to imagine his friend Manuel growing up there. He could see it. He could picture the man as a small boy running into the chilly waters of the lake, and going with his father out on the boat to fish. Nile could imagine that boy helping his dad spread out the nets to dry and then moving through them with needle and rope to mend them. Titicaca was a place where a man like Manuel Negara would have been happy.

Barrabas and Bishop walked toward the structure. Nile wondered what had become of the young Bolivian officer since their time together in Vietnam. There had been many friends like Manuel who'd disappeared from Nile's life. If Barrabas had led the usual kind of life, a man with a steady job, perhaps a family and wife, then his old friends could have written him at his home address in some suburb, and they could have gotten together for beers and barbecue every year or so. Their families would have joined the party, and maybe a few of them would have all gone on vacation together.

If Nile Barrabas had lived the usual kind of life, that is. But those were parts of life that Nile would never know— had never really known. There were times, such as the present time, when he actually saw the way that other men whom he'd known might go about their lives, making him wonder what it would have been like to be that way.

But the imagining never helped. It never made any difference. Because Nile Barrabas wouldn't have been the person he was if any of those possibilities had been real. They weren't. He was trying to picture someone else's existence, not his own.

They came to the front door of the simple cottage and Barrabas knocked and waited for an answer.

The door swung open, and a breathtakingly beautiful woman answered the door. She looked up at him and didn't say a word.

"I'm looking for Manuel Negara," Nile said in Spanish.

"Who are you?" the woman answered in English, surprising the two North Americans, who hadn't expected a person in this fishing village to speak their language.

"I'm an old friend of his . . . from Vietnam."

The woman barely reacted to the message. There was only a slight tic of her forehead in response. "Manuel is not here. He has not been here for a long time. He's gone, I suppose to Peru. Maybe to Paraguay. It could be Brazil. I don't know what border he crossed, or if he even made it."

"Border? He left the country?"

"My husband was on the wrong side of the revolution. It happens to men like him, and like you." There was acid slipping into the woman's voice, and Barrabas felt an icy sensation moving over his skin as he listened to her. He knew what it was because he'd heard it before, when he'd been the one to cause it.

There had been Anna in New York, and there was always Erika, his most frequent companion. He'd heard them both speak like that, with the voice of a woman who has had the misfortune to tie up with a warrior and who then has had to live with her choice—if it was a choice and not a cruel trick of fate.

"I need to reach him."

The woman looked at him with only slightly more interest now. She shrugged. "If you find him, tell him to send money." Two small boys, no more than ten years old, poked their heads past their mother's hips to see the big American with the white-looking hair. They grinned broadly at the newcomer. "The children need it."

Nile reached for his wallet and brought it out. He opened it and was about to give the woman some of the many bills inside when she suddenly spoke with a loud and angry voice. "I don't want American charity. It's you Americans who caused all this. You degenerates with your demand for drugs to poison yourselves have taken away everything that matters to my people! You bring on revolutions, and you take away my husband! You corrupt our government and make it the laughingstock of the world! And you think you can give me money to make up for it? Get out! Leave me alone. I want to bring up my sons without the likes of you around.''

She moved to shut the door, but Barrabas's strong hand blocked it from closing. ''I'm Manuel's friend. I'm not giving you charity, I'm repaying some old debts. I don't belive you, either. Manuel Negara would never have left his children hungry. He wouldn't have left anybody's children hungry. I saw him in Vietnam, and I saw how he treated kids there. He hasn't disappeared, and you know where he is. Tell him 'the Colonel' is looking for him. He'll understand. We're at the tourist inn at the next town up the lake. You know the place?''

The woman wouldn't say yes, but her silence was enough of an answer.

''Tell Manuel I'll be there tonight and tomorrow and the next day and however long I have to wait. If he's in this kind of trouble, I want to help him. Get that word to him. I mean it.''

''What you mean is that you'll take him off to fight again someplace. You aren't going to help me or my children. You're going to get my husband killed.''

''I'm going to keep your husband alive.''

Nile let the woman close the door.

''I'M STILL NOT COMFORTABLE with this location,'' Valdez said to Lennart Moberg as he overlooked the final stages of construction at the chemical plant on the shores of Lake Titicaca, only about fifteen miles away from the fishing village where Nile Barrabas had found Negara's family.

Moberg, who was stooped over a set of blueprints, answered with an air of exaggerated patience. "I've told you, the process demands a huge amount of water. There was no other option. The rivers that feed into the Amazon have too many minerals and other natural pollutants in them. We would have to spend a fortune to purify their water for the project and the technology that would have made it possible would have been prohibitively expensive and difficult to transport.

"But this place is perfect," he finished on a satisfied note.

Valdez hated Moberg for one reason above all else: the man knew about things the general could never understand. He couldn't argue or overrule the Swede, because he didn't even know the words that would have been necessary. He was in control of the government and had started to take a firm grip on the drug traffic by eliminating all but the most necessary and cost-effective exporters, and he was becoming used to the wonderful notion of being the absolute ruler of an entire country. Like most other petty despots, Valdez was frustrated and angered by the idea that there were areas of importance he simply couldn't understand.

He looked down at the Swede and studied the back of his exposed neck and imagined a thick rope around the blond man's skin, stretching the pale flesh enough to produce some good red color.

"Darling," Lucia said, coming up to Moberg and wrapping her arms around his waist, "I want to go back to La Paz soon. We have a dinner at the Venezuelan embassy tonight."

"We may have to be late, Lucia," Moberg said as he straightened up. "I have to make sure that everything is going as planned here, or else we'll fall behind schedule."

"But the plant's almost done now. You'd sent the necessary instructions ahead months ago, and the workers have been at it ever since. Why must you stay here now?"

Valdez felt annoyed again. His sister had shown altogether too much affection for Moberg. "Go with her," he said sharply, glad to have something he could tell the Swede to do. "She's right—you are of little use at the current stage. The main work that must be done is military. I have to construct a more substantial defense perimeter for the plant.

"I'm beginning to make the drug dealers anxious. At first they were happy that I had eliminated so many of their small competitors. They thought I'd be happy to just give them a clear field to play. They're starting to realize that I might want to take care of some of them, as well, and they're not pleased.

"They have private armies, and they have access to more resources if they want them. Some of them have been making more money than the national government in the past few years. The main concern at the moment is to make sure the plant is secure. And that—" Valdez was happy to be able to say "—is my responsibility. What has to have precedence now is my work.

"I'll be here if you need me. You two go to La Paz and to your dinner."

Moberg hesitated for a moment, but then broke into a smile. "I'm surprised that a fancy meal in the city could mean as much to you as a chance to play with such big guns, Lucia."

She took the comment as a friendly joke. "But, darling, they're not loaded yet. They're no fun this way. They're simply pieces of metal. Until there's something intriguing to do with them, I'm not interested at all."

"Then come back tomorrow," Valdez said officiously, wanting to show his own expertise. "They'll be ready by dawn."

"Let's do it, then," Moberg said much too taken with Lucia to be aware of the undercurrent of anger Valdez was feeling. "The city!"

Valdez watched his sister and her new foreign boyfriend as they walked toward her car. He wondered vaguely whether he should let the Swede live after the plant was built, just to keep her company. Lucia could be very difficult if she didn't have whatever plaything she wanted.

She was, after all, his sister, and they had many things in common.

NILE BARRABAS STOOD on the beach in front of the Swiss Inn. The hostelry seemed a strange thing to find in South America, until Barrabas remembered more about the history of the continent.

Most Americans have romantic notions of Hispanic settlers intermixed with natives. According to the American media, all of South America is Spanish-speaking and all of its people have olive skin. That impression is heightened because that is essentially true of the countries closest to the United States and with whose people the United States most often interacts, such as Mexico, Puerto Rico and Colombia.

But the southern half of South America has an ethnic mix much like North America's. There are many Germans, Italians and people from the British Isles in nations like Argentina, Paraguay and Brazil. There is an even larger percentage of Northern Europeans in Chile. Some of that mix had seeped over the border into Bolivia.

The inn was owned by a young Swiss couple who had moved there to escape the ratrace of industrialized urban life. They had picked a violent land to move to—their homework on politics hadn't been the most complete—but they had been lucky enough to find a location in Bolivia that took them out of the roller-coaster ride of La Paz, at least.

There, a hundred miles from the capital, they entertained foreign tourists and a few diplomats on assignment to Bolivia. They weren't even aware, Nile had noticed, that they had simply transported their yuppie life-style to a different geographic location. Just like the young professionals who retire early to Maine or Oregon, thinking they're brave frontiersmen, when in fact they are the same as before and only happen to breathe some better air than the rest of the yuppies.

Out on the lake, Barrabas could see a small flotilla of fishing boats working in the moonlight. The primitive craft sported unused outboard motors. The stiff lines of the mechanical devices looked weird on the simple boats and were evidently the fishermen's only concession to modern times. They weren't worried about state-of-the-art fishing techniques, that was obvious. They were still practicing the method of their ancestors, just as they had for centuries before the Spaniards had appeared. The fishermen were throwing out their huge seines, nets that hang vertically in the water because one side is weighted and the other is suppled with floats.

It was nearly midnight. Nothing had happened. The heavy meal he and Geoff had shared at the inn was a ball in his stomach. He knew that Manuel would show up or send word, but when? And why had he ever run away?

Barrabas thought about the circumstances under which he'd allow himself to be forced into hiding. It wasn't that hiding was such a terrible thing. It could simply be a strategy. Only a fool would refuse to recognize the importance of retreat in the creation of a military plan.

He continued to theorize. What would possibly make him go underground in his own country? What conviction or danger could possibly force him to leave his family behind—if he had one?

The faces of Manuel's two little boys came through clearly in Nile's mind. The image brought a pang of private emotion to him—one that no one else in the world would ever see.

It was time to give up, Nile decided as he checked his watch once more. If Manuel were going to come, it would be tomorrow.

Barrabas turned and began to walk up the stairway to the inn. One of the waitresses was standing outside a side door that, Barrabas assumed, led to the kitchen where she probably worked and from which she was taking a break. She was dressed for the cool evening of the high elevation with some kind of padded jacket covering her upper body.

When she saw him ascending toward the inn, she began to move toward him. He caught a glimpse of her face in the moonlight and remembered that she had been the prettiest waitress in the dining room when he and Geoff had eaten. The admission of her charms didn't mean that he had any interest in her now. He did the same quick calculation he always went through when he thought a woman was interested in him, and he decided that he was much too distracted to enjoy a dalliance.

"*Señor*," the girl said with a lilting accent as they came closer to each other, "you are the one they call 'the Colonel'?"

The use of that nickname stopped Nile in his tracks. "Yes." There was only one person in Bolivia outside the team who would think to call him that.

"Then I have to ask you to wait for a moment before you go into the house. There is someone who would like to talk to you."

Nile followed the girl back down the slope to the water. Once they were at its edge, she pulled something out from the folds of her bulky coat. Nile recognized it as the kind of signal that the coast guard used to communicate with other boats with a minimum of interference. It was essentially an oversize flashlight, but the beam was focused with great intensity by the folding armatures she was just clipping into place. The device had a reflective inside coating that multiplied the power of the battery-powered beam she had just turned on.

The light was obviously directed to the fishing fleet Barrabas had been watching earlier. The girl clicked the switch of the flashlight a few times, evidently in some kind of code.

Nile looked out over the water and saw that one of the boats was dragging in its nets. As soon as they'd been gathered onto the deck of the craft, the boat went through a sudden transformation. A facade fell from it, revealing an interior that was much different from its former appearance.

Big chunks of what seemed to be an outer casing revealing a fast inboard motorboat. While the other men gathered up the discarded wooden facade, which had floated readily, the boat's engine revved up quickly, the noise breaking the calm of the lake. In a matter of seconds, the sleek craft was skimming over the surface of Titicaca, heading directly to them.

The pilot was highly skilled, and the motor was deceptively powerful. The boat took less than five minutes to reach land, then the engine was cut to allow the boat to slide up onto the sandy bank without damaging the hull. As soon

as it did, a man in a traditional Bolivian costume climbed
over the foredeck and then jumped up onto the ground.

"Pretty good cover, huh, Colonel?"

"Manuel!" Nile grabbed his friend by the shoulders, and
the two men embraced each other briefly. "What the hell is
this all about?"

"The others are from my village. That camouflage
wouldn't stand up if you got close to us, but from a distance it's perfect. No one can tell the difference. Since those
are my people, they're not about to squeal on me. With their
help, I have access to any part of the coastline on the lake.
Spies never had it so good before."

Nile realized that two men had been in the boat all along
as Manuel turned to speak first to them and then to the
woman. One of the men got out onto solid ground just long
enough to help push the craft off from the shore. Then he
scampered back onto it, and the pilot fired up the engines
once more. In a matter of seconds, as quickly as they'd
come in to shore, they were back out on Titicaca, heading
for the fleet and the safety of their cover.

The young woman led the North American and the Bolivian back up the hill to the inn. The three of them slipped
into the kitchen, which was empty. She explained that the
guests and other servants had either gone to bed or to another resort for a big party, and they could feel free to talk
there as long as they liked.

She produced a bottle of good Argentine wine for them,
uncorked and poured it, then disappeared.

"What the hell are you here for?" Manuel demanded as
soon as she'd left. "I never thought I'd see you in Bolivia."

"There's stuff going on here that I'm involved with,"
Barrabas answered as he took a sip of his wine.

"You?" Negara seemed suddenly crushed. "You're involved with drugs?"

"Fighting them," Barrabas said.

Negara relaxed immediately and looked sheepish about his assumption. "I should have known. Forgive me. But if you'd seen what's happened to so many good men down here in the past few years..."

"It takes an awful lot to fight off the temptation cocaine represents when it's in such enormous quantity as Bolivia's trade with the United States."

"You'd have thought, Colonel, that some of them wouldn't have gotten involved. You'd have thought they were so good that they'd resist what you call 'the temptation.' But one by one, most of the good men in our military have given in.

"It's like we saw in Vietnam, where the South Vietnamese patriots were the best men we knew—in the beginning. But then, after countless missions against a ferocious enemy, they'd come back to Saigon, and time after time they'd find the politicians robbing the country blind.

"You remember, don't you, some of the men that turned to the black market? It happened, a lot, when they'd lose their best friends in a battle because they had run out of ammunition. Their quartermasters had sold most of it to international arms dealers with the help of the kingpins in the government.

"The good guys couldn't take it. They couldn't take the sacrifice they were making and the contrast between that and what the rest of the country was doing.

"It was the same thing here. One by one, the best officers gave up. They just stopped caring. They'd try to do their job and they'd go after the worst offenders, but it didn't work. Everything really went down the tube after you Americans began to send your army in. It was the first time foreign troops had ever been in the streets of La Paz. It was the rape of the country's honor. It seemed as though we were an occupied land.

"I understood a lot more about the Vietnamese after the day I saw a U.S. Army Huey helicopter armed to the teeth land at the international airport and a dozen American infantrymen climbed out of its belly."

Barrabas said nothing. He understood the hurt in Negara's patriotic pride, but he also understood something much more important: Negara hadn't broken. That was the key to the situation. In the worst of human sewers, there was human nobility. Bolivia's best example of a good man was sitting across the table from him.

"I thought we had a chance to bring it together with Martinez," Negara finally began again. "That dream isn't over. We at least kept him alive after the coup. He's over in Peru. Hiding. The president of the republic is being kept in the attic of a ramshackle old house.

"He's ready to give it up, go back to teaching, probably move to the States where he can get a cushy job at one of the Ivy League colleges, where they're big on refugee politicians. He'd like to be a man of principle and a man of historic dignity. He's the only hope we have. But he's not the strongest individual in the world. He doesn't understand fighting slime like Valdez, the way you have to meet their treachery head-on. He's not sure we can fight the man anyhow. I don't have much time to convince him otherwise."

"What are you going to do?" Nile asked.

Negara smiled, "I'm going to kill the bastard Valdez, what do you think? I'm going to get him and his body guard. The country is in shambles. No one else is in a position to get into power. Martinez will be a breath of fresh air to almost everyone. The people didn't hate him. Valdez made an error in judgment: he can't make it look as though

Martinez was a fuckup. The country was actually moving—if only slowly—and people were beginning to realize it.

"Valdez and his sister are trying to pull a Perón and Evita act on the peasants—telling them that they are the saviors of the lower classes. They might pull it off, if they have long enough, but it hasn't taken yet. Martinez was doing the work that *had* to be done to try to get Bolivia back on its feet economically and socially, and that hurt a lot of folks. But most people understood how bad the trouble was that we were in. The picture they're trying to paint of Martinez now won't stick. He wasn't bad enough. Everyone knows he certainly wasn't evil. Bolivians *know* what 'bad' is in a government.

"The new regime has made a mistake by frightening the middle classes, what's left of them, and by turning off the small-time hoods. Valdez has moved too soon to gain credibility, and among too select groups of people. If we can ever move, the restoration of the Martinez democracy won't be opposed by the majority of the people. They'll welcome it."

" 'If'?" Barrabas asked. "What's the issue?"

"Valdez. He has to go. I told you that. And with him has to go his sister. We're proving how dangerous it is to let a deposed leader operate from outside the country. She's beautiful, and she could turn into the kind of star that Evita Perón was in Argentina. If she got to Chile and convinced the fascists there that she was on their side—that her anticommunism was the same know-nothing shit as theirs—they could let her broadcast into our country, give her a base of operations, lend her military support somehow, all of it.

"The other issue? We have to move quickly. There's a plant going up on the shores of the lake, just north of my village. No one understands what it's actually for, but the word is out that Valdez is coming up with something so big that he'll have the money and the power to rule Bolivia for the rest of his life. If he has enough cash to throw around to the poorest of the miners and the peasants, then he'll have their allegiance, after all. And if he can actually use money to do away with the criminal elements on the streets of La Paz and the other major cities, even the middle class will come to respect him.

"If Valdez isn't stopped soon, he won't be stopped."

Nile Barrabas looked at his friend seriously for a while and then began to smile. "Oh, don't worry about your man Valdez, Manuel. He's going to bite the big one, soon. I'm going to help him do it." Barrabas maintained his smile while the words he'd just heard echoed inside his head: there's a plant going up on the shores of the lake...no one understands what it's actually for....

"Let's have some more wine, Manuel, and then we're going to do some talking."

11

Lee Hatton walked through the door of the suite. Nate Beck had moved the headquarters of the SOBs' action up to the suite on the top floor of the International. In only a couple days, he'd transformed the once elegant rooms into an electronic marvel.

Every available tabletop space seemed to be taken up with computers, modems, printers, scanners and transmitters of all sorts. The high-tech sounds echoed against the walls. There was the soft *click click* of the computer keyboards while Nate typed, the monotonous mechanical pounding of the printers and the various *beep-beeps* of the receivers and other communication gear.

Lee dropped her valise on the first empty chair and walked into the second room, where Nate was working. She had on a businesswoman's severely tailored suit that left her feeling uncomfortably bound up. Her hair was tied back in a tight bun. She seldom wore makeup and people even more seldom noticed, but seen framed in the starkness of the rest of her appearance, her uncolored face made her look as though she had spent her entire life behind a desk. There was nothing to suggest her athletic activities, certainly nothing to even hint that she was a member of an elite mercenary team.

"Nate, what the hell are you doing?" Lee asked when she walked up behind the SOBs' electronic specialist and saw him glued to a computer monitor. It was one of the new high-resolution screens, with more resolution than most televisions on the domestic market.

But the monitor's images had nothing to do with computerized data retrieval or telecommunications. Instead, it was displaying some kind of futuristic cops and robbers show.

"Lee! Oh! Ah!" Beck jumped up and immediately switched off the screen. "Nothing, just doing some—"

"Was that an *American* television program you were watching?" Lee asked.

He calmed himself down and retreated behind a cool, fake facade. "Well, I was doing some hacking with these new machines I've been working on. You know I had set up a communications link with Jessup's office in New York, just for the information we had to get from the States right away, and that new assistant in his office, the one who handles these things—"

"In the middle of this assignment, the two of you have rigged up a way for you to get television programs imported from thousands of miles away?" Lee began to laugh. The idea of Beck doing that seemed just too impossible. The man had to have his toys, and he had to play his games.

"It was the *Max Headroom Show*, the only thing worth watching on the tube. It's a hacker's dream come true."

Lee went about loosening up after a day of going checking up on the export/import firms of La Paz, helping it all along with a good gin and tonic, while Beck proceeded to passionately explain the idea of the television series based on a character who lived inside the world of computer chips and access codes.

"Nate, stop!" she finally demanded when, drink in hand, she'd collapsed into one of the hotel's comfortable overstuffed chairs. "It's fine. Everyone on the team knows you're getting your job done. You always have and you always will. If a simple television program will make you happy and you think you have the time to arrange this high-tech transmission, go for it!''

"Well—" Beck paused for a moment and blushed slightly. "Just don't tell the guys, will you? I'm not sure they'd understand." He became very serious again. "And do not tell Nile."

"Don't worry, the colonel will never know that you pulled this off," Lee assured him. She understood his concern. The most important part of Nile Barrabas's leadership was the way he made all of them want to live up to every expectation he had of them. He was a strong man, a powerful personality, and he wouldn't ever browbeat the team members into anything. Still, somehow he left them feeling the need to excel and made them desperate not to disappoint him.

"What's up with your work?" Beck asked, taking advantage of the opportunity to change the subject.

"Lots of walking. Lots of talking to traders who would have loved a tumble in the hay. Lots of figures and statistics. Even more of a void."

"Nothing?"

"Well, there's something that might make sense...." Lee let her voice trail off for a while, then decided to share her speculations with Beck. "If it's true that there is no more of the regular distillation of cocaine going on here—or very little—that means certain kinds of chemical shouldn't be in demand. There are only so many uses for some of the materials going into the traditional manufacture of cocaine."

"Yeah?" Beck said, pulling up a desk chair and straddling it backward to face her. "So, go on."

"There have been major imports of ether in Bolivia. It's a very unstable chemical, and one that's essential for the production of cocaine from the coca plant. There's absolutely no other use for it in those amounts in Bolivia that I can understand.

"But I was in the offices of the São Paulo Corporation today, one of the big Brazilian import/export firms, one that did some work for Jessup once."

"I remember, I got the address for you with the name of the contact from the Fixer's files when you started this."

"I spoke to the contact—a decent guy, one of the few that didn't think it was a sin for a woman to be in some trade other than prostitution—and he told me that they'd handled the transportation of massive quantities of ether into Bolivia for some of their clients as recently as this week, *and* that there'd been a major reorder by the government itself."

"But they're not supposed to..."

"But it would make sense, Nate. Whatever the structure of this artificial cocaine, the process might end up with the production of a synthetic that is more like coca in its natural state, rather than like the final form of cocaine. If that's true, then the traditional means of manufacture would still have to be used from that point on."

"What does that mean to us?" Beck asked.

Lee looked at her empty glass and thought for a minute before answering. "It means that we should tell Nile to be very, very careful, because the quantities of ether we're talking about might be enough to blow the roof off the Andes. Ether is very explosive. If it were more stable, we'd use it in our armaments. It could give dynamite a run for its money, pound for pound."

"Hell," Nate said, "we forget that some of the old-fashioned stuff is just as strong as the new."

"And just as dangerous," Lee added. "The strength of a rattlesnake's venom didn't diminish just because we discovered cyanide. That snake bite can still kill you, and make you very, very dead.''

LIAM O'TOOLE and Claude Hayes had changed their clothing—at least three times a day. The bills at the haberdasheries where they were shopping had been limited only because not that many very expensive outfits were available in their large sizes. Liam O'Toole had thought that would put a damper on Hayes at first, but he'd overlooked the most obvious alternative:

"Yes, yes, General Estaban, I think you're right. There are only so many great character roles left in the modern cinema.'' While Hayes was speaking to the general on the telephone, a team of tailors were swarming around him. Wearing only his briefs, he made sure that the men could get all the measurements they needed as quickly as possible to copy the high-fashion men's clothing featured in the advertisements in magazines such as *Interview* and *GQ*.

O'Toole would have liked to make fun of his pal, but he couldn't. He, too, was standing in his underwear while tailors were going crazy all around him.

This plan was impossible, O'Toole told himself once more. But he hadn't been able to make himself believe that, because it was working like a charm.

General Estaban and a score of other Bolivian officers had been lunched, dined, cocktailed and breakfasted in a nonstop campaign orchestrated to perfection by Claude Hayes. The two Americans had presented themselves as ultimately stylish and successful movie people. The frequent changes of clothes and the way they'd been throwing around money made the characters they were playing seem all the more convincing.

As a result of the blitzkrieg of hype that Hayes had thrown at them, the Bolivian army men were, to a one, convinced that they were being offered their one and only chance at becoming movie stars.

The country had offered their one and only chance at becoming movie stars.

The country had proven a treasure trove of aspiring Tom Cruses and Patrick Swayzes. Not that youthful stars were their only options. Far from it. There were many older statesmen who would have liked to challenge General Estaban for the "mature" lead.

General Estaban was sure he had secured his position lately by undergoing an amazing transformation. His hair had been ever-so-slightly dyed—not to give it any color, but to make it a more pure white. The kind of leader he should portray should be old, and attempting to appear younger than his years—if it made him less usable to the producers—was a luxury he was glad to give up.

The general had also started to wear even more carefully tailored and pressed uniforms once he'd seen how much the Americans put into their dress and appearance. A man of his stature couldn't afford the stylishness the two supposed citizens of Hollywood pretended to, but he could make sure he attained their image of what a general should look like.

There was even a question in O'Toole's mind whether the general was inventing some new medals. There certainly were more pieces of brass and ribbon on Estaban's chest than there had been when the whole foolish business had started.

How did I get into this? O'Toole wondered as a fussy tailor held out a just-sewn pair of raw silk slacks for him to step into. What did *this* have to do with trying to be a poet?

But, damn! It *did* work.

At every meeting they "took" with every person in the military, the same script had been played out. There would be an item that the general had promised for their use, and which demand the officer they were talking to insisted was impossible.

One colonel had told them that they couldn't possibly have use of three of the F/A-18 jet fighters that the Bolivian air force had just received from the United States. Hayes got hard-assed and demanded the planes, threatening to move the entire production to another country and to blame the officer for the cancellation of Bolivia's part in the enterprise.

The threat was O'Toole's cue in those situations, and he would begin to wonder out loud about the possibility that the pilot might be exactly the one they were looking for to take a major role in the film. Didn't Hayes think the air force officer had a natural affinity for the camera?

Hayes would never give in easily to O'Toole's suggestion, but at that point in the conversation he'd begin to throw around Malcolm MacMalcolm's name.

The combination of the chance at stardom and the idea that the stardom would begin with a partnership with the great celebrity was too much for any of them to pass up.

The air force colonel hadn't been an exception. He couldn't stop himself from dreaming about his face on the screen during Top Gun. The possibility of immortality was too appealing, too wonderful! The planes suddenly became available. The final arrangements were made, along with the times for the crews to be at the landing strip.

And so it went with M1 tanks and just about any other matériel that the duo demanded for the props of their film.

Where were the other stars? Where was the rest of the production crew? Why weren't there any cameras yet? Occasionally those questions would come up, and Hayes would handle them all with a blast of indignation for fools who didn't understand the "cinema." That was not the way that Malcolm MacMalcolm worked!

Would Liam O'Toole ever have allowed things to reach such a point if there weren't an element of revenge against MacMalcolm involved? He wondered about that again as the tailor helped him put on the new satin shirt that had come fresh from the sewing machine.

O'Toole groaned when he realized it was one of those shirts that only had a single button, barely above his navel. The bare chest was going to be stylish that night, which also meant he'd have to wear all the gold chains they'd accumulated to show them off against his flesh.

He hated it. But, he thought, shaking his head in dread, it was going to work. It had worked every time so far. The flashier the men, the more likely they were to be from Hollywood. The more ostentatious, the better for the image. He'd been suckered into the whole idea of the movies himself. Why should he be so surprised that other guys were doing the same thing? O'Toole shook his head again as the tailor produced a jacket that looked as though it came straight from the dressing rooms of *Miami Vice*. The hardest task the tailors had faced all day was making the brand-new garment appear casually wrinkled to fit the present-day trends.

Hayes finally hung up the phone. The tailors who had finished clothing their charges accepted the big payment the black man offered them and gratefully bowed themselves out the door.

"Well, O'Toole, that was the last one. We have a coastal patrol boat on Titicaca ready if Nile needs it. We've covered all the bases there are, guy. When we finish up with this party tonight, we'll be home free."

"Damn, Claude, I want out of this. I came down here to be a goddamn fighter and leave all this shit behind. I want some action."

"My man," Hayes joked, "when was the last time you took a trip with the good Colonel Barrabas and didn't see action?"

THE WATERS OF TITICACA were surprisingly chilly.

Barrabas understood that it was only cultural conditioning that made him expect that it should be warmer. All of South America was supposed to be warm, even hot, tropical. His mind wanted the whole continent to be one big steaming Amazon basin. But the Andes were some of the highest mountains in the world, and the height meant that the lake was fed by snow and glacier-swollen mountain streams.

It had already taken him all of their stay to get his breathing back to normal. The oxygen levels were so much lower than they were used to back in the States that the human body had to have that time to acclimatize itself. Even in the rock-hard shape that Nile kept his body tuned, he had had to recondition it for this altitude. He now understood just why American and Canadian Olympic athletes went to the Rockies to train. If their muscles could take the rigorous workouts at those altitudes, when they got back down to normal elevations, they would be in the best shape possible.

Swimming is one of the most difficult sports to adjust to. Always the best kind of conditioning, with its combination of aerobiclike stress and its use of almost all the muscles in the body, swimming makes the greatest demands on humans. Anybody who could swim a long distance that high up in a mountain range could do wonders in a pool at sea level.

Right then, Barrabas felt ready for the Olympics himself. Dressed carefully in a wet suit to protect his body's temperature from the cold waters of Titicaca and wearing an oxy-

gen tank for any underwater forays, he was moving through
the water with his Bolivian friend. Propelled by heavy, long
flippers whose action multiplied their bodies' power, they
sped quickly through the dark lake. They hadn't gone underwater yet; it hadn't been necessary. They had assumed
there would be some kind of coastal patrol, but there
weren't any government boats to be seen.

He and Manuel Negara had to check out the new factory
that was causing so much excitement among the members
of the new regime. The land approaches were being carefully guarded. They already knew that there were so many
infantrymen on duty that they would need an army of their
own to attack from that direction. The dangers of a surveillance mission from the land side were too great to risk when
they had the option of the water approach.

Manuel's villagers had proved themselves loyal and able
allies. They were obviously proud of their native son and his
position in the Martinez government, both when it had been
in power in La Paz and in exile in Peru. They had also lost
any trust they had in other governments in the capital. There
had been too many mean-spirited ones for the villagers to
ever bother with. If their own Manuel would tell them they
must do something, though, they were going to follow.

Barrabas and Manuel were coming up to the shore now.
They carefully stood up only enough to get a foothold on
the lake's bottom, keeping only their heads above the surface. Staying as low as they could for as long as possible,
they moved toward the firm land. When they were forced to
bend over completely, they moved to float in to shore on
their bellies.

On land, they shed their tanks, flippers and the heavy wet
suits that were now a burden. Though the night air was cool
each had only cotton clothing underneath. But personal
comfort wasn't a current concern of theirs.

The two men moved in the direction of the plant, then suddenly Manuel fell on his stomach and motioned to Nile to come closer. When Barrabas was up beside him, the Bolivian pointed to the well-lighted industrial complex in front of them.

"Our intelligence has been so poor because Valdez has used only his most trusted troops as laborers. He even had to stop work on this project, we discovered, when he carried out his coup. He needed those men for the struggle, and we hurt his schedule with our resistance, which he hadn't really expected.

"The men are all drawn from outlying regions, El Beni and the Chapare. They've been fed a line by Valdez about their future and the way he's going to protect them. They've believed him. Their natural distrust of other people in the country has kept them quiet, making them good servants to the dictator. They believe, with good cause unfortunately, that the traditional powers in La Paz are their families' oppressors."

Barrabas took all that in, but he was much more interested in the sight in front of him. It was obvious that the construction was nearly done. The heavy equipment—bulldozers, levelers—was all parked off to a side with tarpaulins covering them.

A number of men appeared to be engaged in highly skilled work—pipe fitters, engineers of different kinds—hurrying about the site. There were no common laborers, though. The plant was a maze of large bent tubing, stainless steel holding tanks, loading platforms for an obviously new rail spur and huge pipes leading from the lake.

Nile couldn't get a complete count of the number of uniformed soldiers who were swarming all over the place, engaged in something, but not in construction.

Then, just as he was trying to figure out the problem, he heard the unmistakable sounds of approaching tanks. A line of M1s came into view, and the terrifying noises of metal wheels clashing against metal treads filled the night air.

"Damn," Nile said when he saw the number of them. "That has to be the entire Bolivian armed capability."

Manuel agreed. "You have to remember, there really isn't any real threat to our borders. The South American countries keep up a massive arms race, but it's mainly for the sake of macho self-image. There's no one we could ever use the material against. See what happened when Argentina tried it with the Brits? The major powers like to sell arms to us because of the profits, but their international policies aren't going to let the use of those arms get out of hand.

"Valdez can afford to use all of his resources here, at least for now. We haven't been able to set up a resistance to his regime yet. I don't know if the democratic forces in Bolivia will be able to do that for months yet."

"They have the best, just about," Barrabas noted. "Those are the new TCM 105 mm armored guns on their turrets. The machine guns mounted externally on the commander's cupola are 7.62 mm."

Barrabas turned to Manuel with sudden understanding. "Are those the machines you said you and your men held off?"

"Yes," Manuel said bitterly. "We could only barely do it. We had to get President Martinez on to his helicopter, and then some of the rest of us got out, as well. The holding action was the most we could perform against that.

"We only had TOW missiles to work with. They were effective, at least as efficient as anything else to send against M1s with those armaments, but we couldn't really have beat them.

"We did as well as we did only because we were up against such poorly trained troops that time. I'd gotten the cadre I commanded up to peak after some hard work at drills and also after having weeded out a hell of a lot of candidates to get a crew that would know how to follow orders and how to stand up against an enemy.

"But there was only so much we could do."

There was bitter defeat and hurt in Manuel's voice. Nile looked at his friend. "You did better than anyone else could have. I know that."

Manuel shrugged off the compliment. The words didn't really help: Nile knew, deep down, that they wouldn't make a difference until Manuel had a victory to replace the shame of his loss.

The two men looked back to the line of M1 tanks. "God, this is going to be hell," Barrabas said. He was considering the situation with renewed interest because of the deployment of the M1s they were now witnessing.

"I didn't know Valdez had the smarts," Manuel said as he watched the tanks disappear, one by one, into bunkers spread around in a circle around the factory. "Do you think he's on to you? Why else would he go so far as to turn the tanks into heavy—but stationery—artillery?"

Manuel had just actually described the reality of the situation. The bunkers were heavily protected shells that turned each one of the armored vehicles into a heavy fortification. Their motors were being cut, and a calm was returning to the lakeside night. Once they were all in their little cocoons, it was going to take even heavier artillery to get them out.

"My men are on the job. They'll come up with what we need to take care of these assholes. I trust them, Manuel. You can, too."

"Let's get out of here," Manuel said in response.

The two men walked crab style away from their perch, back toward the lakeshore. After crossing the three hundred yards of terrain quickly, they were brought up short just before they ran into serious trouble.

Two uniformed guards were standing over their diving gear. Although everything had been well hidden in the foliage, something must have attracted the sentinels' attention.

The two men were speaking, but were still far away and their voices were too low to be understood. The Bolivian soldiers, each armed with an M-16, seemed to visually search the area around them, as though looking for an easy explanation for the presence of the air tanks and the wet suits.

"We've got to take them out," Nile said softly.

"You get the one on your side," Manuel responded.

The limitations they were working under were perfectly apparent to both of them. The one thing they couldn't afford was to let any kind of alarm sound. Their attack was going to have to be silent, and it was going to have to be fast.

The Bolivians had returned their attention to the diving gear and were playing with the controls of the air tanks. There was a faint *whoosh* that Nile and Manuel could only just hear. It was the sound of their vital oxygen escaping uselessly into the atmosphere. They realized that they would have to swim back to the waiting boats far into the lake without the benefit of going under water for protection. If an alarm were sounded, they would be sitting ducks for any water or air search sent out after them.

The two men didn't say anything more to each other but began to move with catlike grace toward their targets. Their only armament consisted of bowie knives in waterproof sheaths attached to their belts. They hadn't planned on such an encounter.

One of the guards was talking more loudly, and Manuel and Nile both knew he was insisting that the incident be reported at once. The other was trying to talk him into waiting just a bit longer. He wanted to paw through the cache of goods some more, just to see if there wasn't something more that would be worth taking with them as private profit.

That bit of greed was going to be the undoing of both.

Nile and Manuel had made it to the top of a small rise, which stood behind the shorefront beach area. They were only about three feet higher than the sentries, but that was enough to give them a vital advantage, especially with the element of surprise that they had working for them. They both sprang at once for the men.

The knives were held outstretched before them. Nile felt himself going through a mental transition that stunned him. He was remembering the way the men had talked about the jaguar being the only animal that hunted human beings. Suddenly he felt as though the knife he was carrying wasn't a manufactured piece of metal, but a part of himself.

Nile felt the rush of something animal in himself, something savage that was about to be released. When he and Manuel suddenly leaped forward in unison, with those sharp knives at the ready, it seemed to him that they were actually beasts who were pouncing on their prey with their claws unsheathed for the attack.

The guards didn't have a chance. Most likely they didn't even have time to understand what the sudden and unexpected sounds were. They probably didn't feel the steel enter their jugular veins nor register the warmth as their blood gushed out from that most vulnerable spot in a man's body.

The knives cut through the skin, the neck gristle and the bone, the sharp edges powered by the attackers' physical bulk. As soon as Nile and Manuel felt their blades enter the bodies, they pulled sharply up on their handles, letting the knives tear through flesh and unleash an even larger flow of bodily fluids from the two Bolivians.

It was over in seconds. It was done. Nile stood there and felt the adrenaline surging through him, just as it did in any battle. But there was something particularly unique about the one attack, something he was shaken by. Unexpectedly the mental gymnastics that Billy Two had been going through flashed into his mind, and Barrabas wondered if the sensation he had experienced wasn't similar to the one the Osage described when his Hawk Spirit came calling.

It was the way he and Manuel had done the maneuver in such utter synchrony, as though they'd practiced this one thing together all their lives and each had known precisely how it must be done and exactly how the other would do it as well.

Manuel, less distracted, was quickly getting into his wet suit. Nile tossed the ideas out of his mind and started climbing into his own protective gear, which he knew he'd need in the chilled waters of Titicaca.

"Leave the tanks," Manuel said quietly as he and Nile finished putting on their flippers. "They won't come after us for long enough. We can make it to the boats out there in time. They will never suspect the fishermen. They're part of the landscape in Titicaca, always present, never noticed."

The two men moved into the water of the lake without the useless oxygen tanks. They slipped themselves into the water and smoothly began to stroke out toward the waiting fishing fleet.

Nile knew his lungs would be burning with protest by the time they finished their marathon swim. It was going to be a struggle for his body to make it all the way without stopping. He was, of course, in prime shape, and he had been in Bolivia's rarefied atmosphere for many days, but it was still going to be torture on him.

He welcomed it, not only because it was simply another chance to match himself against the elements, but because the physical exertion was going to erase from his mind the images of twin jaguars flying through the air, their fangs and claws ready to rip through human flesh.

12

"You're using up a lot of my basement space, you know. I got stock down there, such as food, booze, and I can't have you turning it into a human warehouse." Maria was downing a morning screwdriver while Billy Two was eating his breakfast.

He didn't even look up at her when he answered. "There's no reason to kill the poor bastards. They were just army slobs doing what they were told to do. Let them stay down there for a while. We should have this show on the road soon enough."

"Yeah, you men all say that kind of thing. Big promises are the specialties of your houses." Maria stood up and went to the counter of her kitchen and pulled the bottle of vodka down from its shelf. She splashed only a little of the liquor in her glass, then went to the refrigerator and filled it with some ice and orange juice.

Billy Two watched her and realized that the drinks were more for show than effect. There was a hint of alcohol in that glass, but not much more. The woman had obviously gotten her impression of how a female bar owner should act from B-grade movies, and she was going to live up to the role.

She rested her haunches against the counter when her drink was made and stared at Billy Two. "You and your friend got problems?"

Billy Two looked up from his scrambled eggs and flashed a puzzled expression at her. "No. Why do you ask that?"

"Just wondering if I was up against turf stuff—you know, pals respecting their buddies' 'property' so much they don't want to make a move and upset the friendship."

Billy Two grinned at her and went back to his food. "Maria, I'm just not interested. Thanks for the compliment. But it's not on the schedule this time around."

She moved closer to him and leaned forward enough for her robe to fall open and reveal a generous glimpse of her breasts. "I could make you happy. You could make me happy. It's not a happy world. We should both do our part to change things."

The big Osage kept shoveling food through his grinning mouth and refused to respond.

Just then, Alex Nanos came into the room to join them. "What a *great* day," he proclaimed. It was for him; he and Maria had gone back and picked up their fun and games in the sack to erase the memory of the earlier interruptions.

Maria smiled at him; her smile was earnest, though just a little tinged with regret. The Greek was handsome, hairy, an energetic lover and an easy companion. Like most women who enjoy a good party, Maria was happy to have had him. She simply wished she'd had the Indian, too.

She looked down at Billy Two, who had finished his food and was drinking thick Bolivian coffee. The Osage was only wearing pants, and his naked, hairless chest seemed a luxurious contrast to Nanos's shaggy hairiness. She imagined how smooth and silky that tanned flesh would be as it rubbed against her, and she could feel what it would be like to...

Juan, Maria's chief bartender, appeared at the kitchen door. "Maria, Pasquale is here!" He'd been already on duty that morning, stocking the bar downstairs and cleaning up after the long night.

Billy Two looked at the man and realized there was fear and concern in his voice and the way he was acting.

"He wants to talk to the North Americans?" The sentence sounded much more like a question than an announcement. Evidently, whoever Pasquale was, Juan didn't understand why Billy Two and Nanos would create any interest in him.

Maria seemed just as unsure. Finally she said, accompanying her words with a shrug, "Bring him up." She turned to the two SOBs and explained, "Pasquale is a small-time hood. Not one of the big exporters that Valdez is lining up with, according to those two soldiers you've got chained in my cellar.

"He's a pal of mine. He's a crook, but an honest one, if you know what I mean."

Juan led a very thin, almost emaciated Bolivian into the kitchen. Pasquale was introduced, and he shook hands with Alex and Billy Two. The formality was obviously artificial for him. When he spoke their names in greeting, his mouth opened to display a set of very rotten teeth, darkly stained as many Bolivians' were.

The natives didn't go for cocaine in the form that North Americans did. They didn't snort the white powder, and few of them understood the root of the slang word for the drug, "snow." To them, the real treat of the coca plant was its leaves, which they chewed endlessly. They didn't give them the same buzz that the processed powder would have, but they sure blunted the edges of life and gave them a very happy disposition. They also ruined their mouths and caused extensive damage to their teeth, besides exposing them to as high a rate of mouth cancer as though they smoked ten packs of cigarettes a day.

They didn't care, and seldom cared about anything when they were chewing a mouthful of coca.

"Pasquale, a drink? Coffee? Something to eat?" Maria asked her new guest.

"No, Maria, thank you. I came here only for one thing." Pasquale sat down on one of the kitchen table chairs across from Billy Two and Alex and looked at the two of them very purposefully.

"We know you had...visitors last night. Many of our own friends have had the same kind of calls—though the endings have been very different from what must have happened here."

"What do you mean?" Billy Two asked cautiously. He wasn't surprised that word about the soldiers had gotten out. At least a dozen of Maria's employees had to have some idea about what had gone on there last night, and such things usually spread quickly through the criminal grapevine. Billy Two wanted more information, especially about those of Pasquale's friends who had received "visitors." The best way to learn was to leave the subject open-ended so the Bolivian could fill in the blanks at his own speed.

"This Valdez, he's making things very difficult for us, for the independents in La Paz. We got things we can do, sure— the girls, the games, the usual stuff—but he's taking away the gravy from our lives, you see? We got friends who have their own private planes and enough balls to fly them between here and the States. It's risky, but the profits...the profits are very, very good.

"We like these men. They come down to La Paz and they pay top dollar, and their dollars are real American ones, not cheap Bolivian pesos. We don't like to see them hustled around by the authorities when there are other, bigger fish in the sea who go free and clear and get special landing rights at the international airports and even at military airfields, for all we know. It's not fair. It's not democratic!''

Pasquale had built himself up to a fevered pitch with the last statement. Billy Two decided not to argue with the man's politics right now. Though, he thought to himself, maybe there was such a thing as equal opportunity for criminals and drug smugglers that should be respected in a republic.

"Why do you want to tell us about that?" Billy Two asked, holding up his coffee cup for Maria to refill with hot brew. "What does it have to do with us?"

"Some of us, we're thinking that maybe General Valdez needs some help remembering the little people of La Paz. Maybe what he needs is a delegation to visit the presidential palace he just moved into to show him the way. And maybe his big-shot friends need some trouble with their lives, just to balance all the easy living they've been having."

"Keep talking, Pasquale," Nanos said, just as interested as Billy Two was. "Tell us how you think the big shots might get hurt."

"Well . . ." Pasquale was edging back a little bit, wondering just how far he should go with the two strangers. But they were obviously friends of Maria's, and the rumors said that they'd done in some of the soldiers who'd been harassing the small dealers.

"The big shots, see, they've let Valdez and the National Guard take all the credit for stopping the flow of the regular cocaine because they got so much of it stored away. They show off to the American press and the American embassy and they're making up for that mess that happened with the U.S. soldiers.

"There've been lots of burnings of coca fields in the Chapare for the television cameras, and the prisons are full of some poor slobs they caught flying in and out of that area in small planes with expensive cargoes. But that's all media hype. It's crap. The peasants, they've been getting money since Valdez came to power. It had been there all along, but the big boys in the government had been skimming it—including Valdez himself.

"Now he's freeing it up, and the poor suckers think he's a god, coming through with the dough they've always heard about but never received. They only know they don't have to work anymore, at least for a while, 'cause they got that cash. So, when Valdez tells them to stop the planting, why not? They got their bills paid, and all of it.

"It looks good. The big exporters, they've been working off this big supply of coke that Valdez stashed away. There are rumors—and I don't get it—that Valdez has some stuff in the background to make sure the supply never runs out. People can't figure that. They don't see much coca being planted or harvested right now, so no one knows how the man expects to keep things going. But that's beside the point.

"The big thing is that a lot of us are hurting, and a lot of our connections have been broken or lost in these damned raids. We need to strike back, or else we're going to go under.

"We just thought you'd like to give us a hand. We know where the big stash is located and just need some guns and a few men who know how to handle them, and we can break into it."

"And then?" Billy Two asked sharply.

"If it all works good, then maybe we're going to take another step, you know? Valdez has only just moved into the presidential palace with that whore of a sister of his. Maybe we'll pay them a welcome call."

Billy Two and Nanos looked at each other. They didn't smile or speak, but they both knew what an opportunity they had been presented with. Their orders were to help find the hidden cache of cocaine, the natural stuff whose location had been a secret. That meant the SOBs wouldn't be very helpful to Pasquale, since they had no intention of letting the white powder go back to the market. But the man and his other allies never had to find out their true purpose. Just striking a blow against Valdez and his heavyweight cohorts would obviously be a victory for these guys. The two SOBs were sure they could help win it for them.

MANUEL STOPPED HIS PACING and swung around to face Barrabas. "Nile, I just don't have the resources for a frontal attack on that factory. You know as well as I do what strong positions those tanks are in now. They are a very real danger in any event, but behind those fortifications, they're impossible for me to handle.

"Only a few scattered loyalists are left in the National Guard. The maybe fifty men I have guarding Martinez in Peru I don't dare move. I only have about twenty-five, trusty able-bodied men in the fishing fleets who are physically capable of fighting and who also know how to handle a rifle."

The Bolivian frowned, then shook his head before continuing. "I don't see how we can go against anything like that setup that Valdez has there.

"We'd be better off hoping for a popular uprising in the streets of La Paz if we can show enough strength there. Even Valdez would have to run if the citizens rose up to greet us. That's been our strategy all along, to work that."

Barrabas shook his head. "Maybe you could pull that off, but I doubt it. The civilian cost of urban guerrilla warfare is too much to risk unless it's absolutely necessary or absolutely sure to work.

"I know that if we take out that plant, Valdez's whole plan will collapse on itself, Manuel. It's the foundation of his strategy. Without it, he'll be lost and then you can move.

"Besides, you may think that the defenses are too much, that's one way to look at that concentration of power. I see it and I get a different take: that's all of Valdez's military strength. From what you've told me and what I've learned from others, that's the core of his own following. Take it away from him, and you only have members of the National Guard and those of the police who aren't committed to one regime or the other, who might be inclined to follow Martinez if there wasn't too much risk to it.

"Valdez has set himself up for us. He's got all his eggs in that one basket, Manuel. We're going to break them and make ourselves a fine omelet."

Manuel was shaking his head disbelievingly, and Barrabas shot him a level look. "You're also underestimating your forces. I've seen them and I've seen their loyalty. They're behind you one hundred percent. There's another thing, and you can't discount it. The National Guard—especially those from landlocked areas like El Beni and the Chapare—have no feel for the sea or large bodies of water. They don't know what the lake can be used for.

"To them, it's nothing. They don't think in terms of boats, or of having to protect themselves from attack from that direction. We saw how they were setting up the defenses: they aren't nearly concerned enough with the lakefront.

"There were only a couple guards in that part of the area last night. The shoreline is the great vulnerability of the defenses, and they don't even know it.

"Those tanks are well protected from land attack, but they're like the big guns the British had in Singapore during the Second World War—they're aimed in the wrong direction. Those cannon were useless to the Brits because they were permanently placed for protection against naval assault. The Japanese just fooled them and came in from the jungle instead.

"We would do the same thing, just reversing the process, coming at them from the waterside instead of from the land. The tanks would be stuck in place, at least for a while. We even have a chance to take them out totally during the attack. I need to check with my command post, but my people may already have the means to turn the balance of power."

Manuel's face acquired an expression of keen interest. "You got more troops here of your own? How many?" he asked. Barrabas hadn't mentioned anything besides a few of his compatriots accompanying him in Bolivia. Manuel had certainly understood they might be mercenaries, but the sudden talk of "command posts" and "people" made everything sound much more interesting.

"I have significant help available to you." Barrabas smiled, wondering if the Bolivian could understand what the small team of SOBs could, in fact, accomplish, and had accomplished in the past. Even a man as good as Manuel wouldn't understand it easily.

If he saw that there were only a few North Americans with Barrabas, he might become unsure again. Nile decided it was better for the Bolivian to have an impression of a team with great power and unequaled strength going to battle beside him.

Besides, it was true. The SOBs were just that.

13

Lee Hatton watched as Nate Beck spoke into the microphone. The special line of communication between the command post in the International and the men in the field had been accomplished with transistorized microwave equipment that Beck had constructed on the basis of some top-secret research and equipment parts secured by Jessup.

Unlike most other microwave communication systems, it didn't require a large dish or antenna, but utilized only a small receiving implement that had fit easily on the terrace of the top-floor suite.

"Got it, Colonel," Beck said, having finishing typing Barrabas's orders into a computer. "I'll get to Claude and Liam as soon as possible. There isn't going to be any trouble, but if there should be, I'll buzz you on that beeper we gave you, and you can check back with me.

"As it stands, just expect that strike at zero-thirty hours, as requested."

The connection was evidently broken. Beck put down his earphones and turned to Lee with a big smirk on his face. "We're going into action!"

"You and me?"

"Nah, sorry, we're the backups this time. The rest of the boys are the ones who're going to have all the fun. We just hold down the fort."

"You said a 'strike,'" Lee asked, working to keep her real emotions from Beck. "Does that mean Geoff's going into action?"

A "strike" probably meant an air attack and anything to do with an SOBs' aerial combat mission usually involved Geoff Bishop. The Canadian was the premier pilot of the team.

"You got it!" Beck said. "That is, *we* got it, if Liam and Claude have done their homework."

"I don't want to just sit here," Lee said sharply. "There must be something for us to do."

"You know better, Lee. There's always someone who has to stay behind the scenes and keep the show working. It's usually my gig, so I know how hard it can be, but the frustration is necessary. We have to have good communications, and the guys have to be able to know that the home base is protected.

"You're out of the arena this one time. Hell, you've had more than your share of fun and games recently. What's the matter, think you'll lose the touch?"

Lee Hatton ignored the joke. She thought back to the party on Majorca and the slippery feel of that fake aristocrat's touch. She wanted something far away from that incident, that was the main thing. She'd played the game of being a society woman, and she'd taken her vacation away from the men. Now she wanted to know she was back with them and one of the group again.

She refused to feel any other emotion, or to even picture Geoff Bishop in aerial combat by himself, without her. That couldn't possibly be anything that would matter to her, she thought, could it?

HAYES AND O'TOOLE were sitting with the two Bolivian air force majors in the dining room of the Ritz Hotel. Each

South American was trying to convince the other that he didn't want a thing to do with anything as crass and unmilitary as a motion picture.

Carlos Miscara was the one insisting on his disinterest the more adamantly of the two. That meant, to the SOBs, that he was more desperate to be in the film.

"It would insult the uniform I wear to protect the fatherland," Miscara insisted firmly.

"But Claude," Liam said, who had his timing down perfectly by that point, "don't you think the way the major's teeth glisten when he speaks is just right? I mean, can't you see the cameras catching the way the light would reflect off them?"

Miscara couldn't help himself. He opened his mouth just enough so the dining room's chandeliers were able to play on his ivories, which were, in fact, very impressive.

One of the scary things in the whole process, to O'Toole, was his own recognition that he might actually be getting good at it. He really was beginning to look and see like a casting director. What if Hollywood had entered his system like some kind of virus and he couldn't get rid of it? He shivered at the very thought.

"You okay?" Hayes asked with concern when he saw the Irishman's body shake.

"Yeah, fine—" Liam paused to regain his composure "—but I'm serious about Miscara. I think we have a role for him."

"We do have a flight scene," Hayes mused.

"Well..." The Bolivian major was fighting to regain ground. The North Americans had moved more quickly than he had thought they would, and it was difficult for him to maneuver himself back into displaying interest after his very recent disclaimers.

"Of course, we now know that the scenes have to be shot tomorrow night," Liam said speculatively. "The two majors here have been very frank about their difficulties in allowing us such short notice for access to their planes."

"That damned bureaucrat the the department of the air force promised us it was all set up!" Hayes was on his high horse again. He, too, was actually getting into the spirit of the thing quite a bit, and it was very annoying that the previously received pledge of cooperation from the administrative officer they'd wooed was being threatened by the two majors who had the real controls over the aircraft.

"I think we must do it," Major Recife announced.

The three other men all turned on him immediately, each one stunned that he'd come through and solved all their problems with that small statement. After implying that Miscara would be the choice for the part in the film, the SOBs expected Recife would be a problem, not an ally.

"It's a question of honor to the fatherland, if in a different sense than that which you see, Miscara," Recife continued. "The country needs this kind of public relations boost. We must show the world that Bolivia isn't a backwater incapable of performing decent acts."

"If you really feel that way, Recife," Miscara said with great relief. "I suppose there isn't a real problem with a single night's flying for the North Americans. After all, they say they only need to do lighting checks and such, take some test shots of the plane in flight to see the kinds of exposures they'll have to make with their cameras...."

"Exactly. When we get to the actual filming, we'll be able to help them all the more thoroughly and more efficiently. Though there is the problem of the flight plan."

"What do you mean, problem?" Hayes asked.

Recife thought for a moment. "There aren't many of those jet fighters in our force, you know. The models you're requesting are the most modern available to South Americans. We've only recently received the few we have, and that only because Valdez was able to show the U.S. Congress that he was serious about the eradication of drugs in the Chapare.

"There are standing orders that they are to be used to guard an installation. The orders come from Valdez himself. I'm afraid you gentlemen will have to be more flexible with your timing, that's all. I've checked the orders, and they call for one of the planes to be in the air at all times in the vicinity of the eastern shore of Lake Titicaca.

"The shifts that have been scheduled mean that one of the planes will be coming in at precisely midnight and being replaced by another. Now, you need landing and takeoff shots, you said. You wanted them at night, in any event. There will be one of each already set up for you at the air base only a few miles from here. Take your pictures that night, save the time and the fuel that would be involved otherwise.

"Miscara can pilot the plane for the takeoff, assuming he's willing to take the midnight to 6:00 a.m. shift in the patrol."

Miscara looked at Recife with sudden dislike. All games about comradeship evaporated at that moment when he understood what his fellow officer was setting up.

Recife, sensing that he was going to lose out on the movie part in any event—Miscara knew the other man was too short, unattractive and swarthy to portray that particular character, and he had bad teeth in addition—he was at least getting back at Miscara. The dreaded midnight-to-dawn flight duty...on a Saturday night!

"Done!" Miscara sneered. What was a single night in the pickup bars of La Paz compared to a lifetime of fame?

The two SOBs could taste their own victory. The pieces were all falling in place. "Hey, waiter!" O'Toole called to the passing man. "Bring us some champagne to celebrate."

"Champagne, hell!" Hayes interrupted. "Just bring us a bottle of that good tequila stuff and some more limes. We're going to party native style."

BILLY TWO DECIDED it was time to call on Hawk Spirit.

They were going to rendezvous with Pasquale's men at midnight. Maria and Alex Nanos were in the bedroom, having a last fling while they could. The creaking of the bed and their moans came through the door to the living room where Billy Two was sitting.

The god was something to be conjured up in his life now, he reminded himself. It was something that should be invited in when necessary. The time before a battle was just such a moment.

Billy Two went to his bags, which they'd retrieved from the hotel after it became obvious that it would be a good idea for both of them to be in the center of action. He pulled out his traveling kit and set it up on the old coffee table before the couch.

Then he squatted on the floor. He had a small mirror, just large enough for the purpose, and he had the paints of his ancestors.

They weren't cosmetics and had nothing to do with the colors that Maria put on her face in deep layers to hide the years and the wear she'd put herself through. The paints were made from natural pigments in the soil and the plants in the lands where the Osage used to roam free and supreme, before the coming of the Europeans.

There were bright reds from certain kinds of soil that had a high iron content and vivid greens from special leaves, a green that didn't fade with age or with mixture with the organic oils of other plants.

Billy Two used to scoff at these things as the toys and dreams of the old men who lived in their memories. He, himself, had grown up in his father's mansion. Billy One had found oil—a whole lot of oil—on his Oklahoma ranch and had brought up his children with plenty of money to spend on many shopping trips to Dallas.

When Billy Two had become older, though, even when he'd only gotten past his teens, he'd gone back to the old men, searching for something more authentic than a million-dollar house with fake-marble toilet fixtures and something more exciting than wondering if the year's new car should be a Lincoln or a Cadillac. Something had been lacking in his existence and, while much had been found when he'd entered the military, a whole dimension was missing for him.

In the chants and the ceremonies of the old men, he'd found a hint of what he was seeking. He'd learned some of the old ways and wanted to learn even more of them. The use of the paints was one of the first lessons he'd had.

Then there'd been that nightmarish stay in the Russian prison and the drugs they'd put into his system. All the other SOBs—and for a while, even Billy Two—had thought he'd been damaged by the awful experience. But as the incident faded into the background and as he got more control over the appearance of Hawk Spirit, Billy Two was more inclined to see it all as something positive.

The trauma of the prison had slammed Billy Two back into the history of the Osage.

He opened the containers of the war paint now. The red was proof of his willingness to draw his enemies' blood. He smeared it over one of his forefingers and drew long diagonal lines down each of his cheeks. Then he wiped the finger and took up some of the green—the symbol of his manhood and his virility. Using the green, he outlined the scarlet bands of paint already on his face.

Next, he drew black highlights around his eyes, which was the mystical manner of the Osage of making themselves appear like the agents of the underworld in order to throw terror into their foes' hearts.

Billy Two made circles around each of his pectorals. They were a taunt to anyone who wanted to shoot him, showing that he didn't fear death in the coming or any other battle, that he offered the opposing marksmen clear targets of his most mortal parts.

He was finished, painted and ready for whatever was going to come to him that night.

He hadn't noticed the way the ceremonial painting had transformed his mind. He hadn't invoked Hawk Spirit and, since there'd been no conscious request for it to be there, he didn't see it. But Hawk Spirit had entered his soul. He was filled with him, protected by him, transformed with him.

"My God," Maria whispered behind him. She had come into the room quietly and seen the reflection of his painted face and chest in the room's large mirror when he'd stood up and come into its range. "What are you?"

"I am Osage," Billy Two said slowly. Then he turned to look at her. She stepped back, a hand held defensively over her mouth. All her toughness was gone, and there was only some mixture of awe and fear there.

Billy Two's face was sliced with sharp-edged, carefully designed chevrons that cut downward toward his mouth. The red, green and black lines were as fearsome as the Japanese Samurai masks. They didn't simply cover his features: they added a dimension to them.

Maria crossed herself. "I'm glad now...I don't ever want that to happen between us."

The Osage warrior said nothing. It wasn't a time to waste fooling with white women. It was a time for a man to prepare himself for battle.

14

"It's all power, Lee," Nate Beck said as he clicked away at his computer. "That's why I love this. Sure, I'm like you, I'd like to be in the field and in the middle of the action myself, but this will do.

"It's not better—that's not the right word—it's just different. I feel like I'm the master of the chessboard up here in the tower. I get the messages from the team members out there, and I'm the one who times the moves, makes them work together.

"And this one! Lee, this one is sheer brilliance. There are the three different maneuvers, all happening at the same time! I've been able to make sure the guys have it down so they act in synchrony with one another. This is going to be one night that Bolivia never forgets, believe you me!

"You know, they named this country after Simon Bolivar, the man who led the revolutionary wars that freed most of Latin America from Spanish colonial rule. He's their George Washington. Well, no one will ever know it because we're never going to tell any historians, but tonight, Nile Barrabas is going to take his own place beside Bolivar in the list of all-time good guys for this country!"

Nate Beck, like all the SOBs, was a man who was in perfect training shape. He was physically able to match the rest of them in terms of his body's abilities on the playing fields, or the fighting fields. But at the moment, sitting at the computers and making the modems hum and the microwave transmitters sizzle, he looked like the most physically inept computer nerd in the world.

Lee Hatton looked on in wonder. The men on the team were capable of such amazing transformations. She, as the group's physician, knew all about the way their minds and bodies worked in tandem.

The one whose psychology was worn on his sleeve was Billy Two, what with his visitations from Hawk Spirit, but she knew that all of them were something more than just ordinary males who went to war. All of them had multiple capabilities, that was obvious, and all of them could change themselves in miraculous ways to meet the needs of the team.

The image of Nate Beck in love with the games he could play on his high-tech gear was just one more example of it.

Lee left her thoughts behind and made one more trip around the suite, checking the locks on the doors and wandering out onto the terrace to make sure there wasn't any suspicious activity going on around them.

Everything seemed secure, and she put her .357 Magnum back in its holster.

Only then did she break into laughter at herself. There she was thinking about how different the men on the team were from other guys, but she hadn't even stopped to consider that it might be strange that a female M.D. was as used to working with a Magnum as she was with a stethoscope.

BILLY TWO LOOKED at the group of men that Pasquale had organized. Hawk Spirit wasn't going to be doing much flying tonight, he realized. His company on the upcoming mission was right out of the gutter.

Just as well, Billy Two thought, becoming fierce, the hawk can live on eating rats if it needs to—it's one of its most common meals.

The fifty lowlife criminals whom Pasquale had gathered in Maria's bar stared at the Osage with deep disbelief. Those chevrons on his face made him look like one of the stone gargoyles that protected the entrances to the ancient Inca temples.

A primitive respect for the American Indian merged with the fear they felt when they saw him. They were, after all, descendents of the Incas. Bolivians have more native blood in them than any of the other former colonies of Spain. They all showed signs of their descent, the wide-set eyes and high foreheads the old people prominent among their characteristics.

Not that they didn't show their current incarnations just as obviously with the ragtag collection of small arms and shifty eyes of common thieves. They were the pimps and dealers of La Paz, the con men and the smugglers. Billy Two wondered whether their occupations were just the result of base greed or if they had been forced into their criminal lives. He wondered if they would have been decent citizens at another time and place, one where they'd been given more opportunities for a full life of constructive work instead of growing up in the poverty and ignorance of the masses in Bolivia, a place where the future seldom looked any better than the bleak present.

He gave up the question, thinking that he'd leave it to the social workers to ponder. All he knew was that he needed a force of men to take out the cocaine supplies that Valdez had accumulated. His talks with Nate Beck had told him that Nile Barrabas was going after the other target with the big guns and that the operation had to be timed with the colonel's.

The aim wasn't merely to confuse the defense forces Valdez had under his command, but they could also make the strike appear even more powerful than it was if it had at least two prongs.

Pasquale was speaking to the group, haranguing them in Spanish. Maria, who'd closed her bar early for the sake of the operation, was giving Billy Two and Alex Nanos a simultaneous translation.

"He's explaining that they've found the stock of drugs in warehouses down by the civilian airport. Now that Valdez himself is handling the exportation of most of the cocaine, there's no need for any games about it, not even silly ones that are only supposed to fool the United States.

"The Americans are all out in the field, working on the extermination of the crops, while Valdez, with his big supplies, is filling the need from the city.

"The planes that are flying the stuff out of here aren't even bothering to hide what they're doing now. They're just going out from the international airport with flight plans filed with the authorities and everything."

The men in the room suddenly broke into raucous laughter. Maria joined them with a loud guffaw.

"They're being stored under the cover of being medical supplies," she said, "and the name of the company is Compassionate Products, Ltd."

Maria and the others became more serious suddenly as they heard the last part of Pasquale's speech. "There are heavily armed guards there, many soldiers with American M-16s and some machine guns are set up as well…M-60s?"

"That'd be what the U.S. sold Bolivia," Alex verified her guess. "It's not going to be fun to go up against those."

"It'll be easy as jumping off a stool," Billy Two announced with a strange grin spreading over his face, and the way his features contorted made his chevrons move and gave him an even more ferocious appearance.

"You know damned well these guys don't just want to beat the other guys and get rid of Valdez. They want that cocaine in the warehouse to sell themselves," Nanos said softly to Billy Two.

"Can't have it. I'm with Hawk Spirit now, and the devil's poisons have to be destroyed. These men, they'll fight anyhow, just to get rid of the competition, and you know they'll do it, Alex. They're after a special kind of revenge. They'll get over the idea of not getting rich, too. I can see it in their faces."

"What you see in their faces is raw fear... of you!" Alex said. "That paint of yours makes it look like someone else is home inside your brain, Billy Two."

"Someone is, Alex. You should know that Hawk Spirit is with me in all ways. He will soar tonight in battle, and he will strike at his enemies with—"

"Yeah, sure," Nanos said quickly, "that's nice, all well and good. I just hope to hell that Claude and Liam have done their job and gotten us the stuff we need to move against these other more earthly problems. Hell! M-60s, all I wanted to hear about."

"Don't worry," Billy Two said just as the men began to chant something in unison, as though they were at a political rally.

"They want you to speak to them," Maria said, her amusement showing in one raised, plucked eyebrow. "They want the barbarian to lead them!"

Billy Two's arms rose in a victory salute, and his shirt spread open to show the paint on his chest. The men roared

with new enthusiasm. Yes! The barbarian was as bad as
Valdez and as strong, but he was on their side.

"GENTLEMEN, ON SUCH short notice!" General Estaban
was horrified by the demands the Hollywood moguls were
making just as he was sitting down to dinner. "Mortars!
Tonight?"

"General," Claude said, "Mr. MacMalcolm is arriving
tomorrow! We just found out. If we don't have the battle
scene in the Andes ready for shooting, he's likely to get right
on his plane again and go back to California. Once he does
that, we may never get him to return to Bolivia."

Estaban was concerned about the way the two Americans were acting. After all their bravado, the way they'd
bullied him in the past, they were suddenly acting very, very
frightened. They appeared to be terrified of the approach of
the big star.

But that only made sense, he realized. Certainly the im-
minent arrival of the man in charge of their jobs and their
livelihood would intimidate them, just as it intimidated Estaban.

MacMalcolm could be made so angry that he would go
and never return? Estaban questioned mentally. Then the
possibility of Estaban's being a star would disappear as well,
he concluded. Mortars? What were a few mortars? There
were piles of them at the National Guard Armory.

"Very well, very well, I will make a phone call. A truck
will deliver them to your hotel tonight, as you request. You
can have them for your six o'clock 'call.'" Estaban loved
using filmmaking lingo like that. He'd been picking up the
little pieces of Hollywood jargon from the two North
Americans whenever he could.

As he picked up the telephone and began to dial, it suddenly occurred to him that none of the other officers in the National Guard or other branches of the service with whom he interacted had simply "had" lunch in the past week. They'd all "taken" lunch with one another or with the producers, using the new word that the North Americans liked so much.

Estaban got through to the supply quartermaster's office and was put on hold while the receptionist rushed to find the commander on duty at that late hour. The general thought some more about the two producers and wondered, just for a moment, how many other members of the Bolivian military they'd been talking to.

Like all the others, Estaban had begged the movie men not to mention his involvement until the very last moment. He and the rest hadn't wanted anyone in the Valdez upper circles to know how free they'd been with their aid. They were waiting till the last moment to make the announcements. As Estaban recalled his own conversation with the two producers, he realized that he'd also overheard some air force men talking about "points" and someone in the coast guard had mentioned "residuals" in another conversation. Were they all involved?

But the general didn't worry for one second about national security in his deliberations. His mind was too consumed with searching its memory cells, trying to remember anyone his own age who might steal the character lead from him. That would be a disaster.

THE VENEZUELAN EMBASSY dinner party was done. Lucia and Moberg shook their hosts' hands and went out the door, where their bodyguard waited for them.

"I wonder what all this movie talk is about, darling?" Moberg asked. "It sounded like the only topic of conversation they had tonight."

"Such things excite people, Lennart, you know that. I suspect there's some production company in town doing a film that had to have mountains. That's the only reason filmmakers have come to Bolivia in the past.

"It does sound interesting, though. If this has any truth to it, there may be some very amusing actors in town quite soon. We'll have to have a party for them at the presidential palace. It would be good public relations for my brother."

"And for you," Moberg said with a smile to his companion, who was obviously pleased with the idea.

The bright-eyed young men from El Beni saluted them sharply, and one of them ran to open the door of the long limousine that was used to transport the couple wherever they went. They climbed into the car, and the door slammed smartly shut.

"A delightful evening," Lucia announced as the driver started to pull away from the elegant building.

"You enjoy all of this very much, don't you?" Moberg asked kindly. The wave of his hands and his eyes let her know that he meant the pomp and circumstance of the life of state they were leading, complete with the guard and on the hood of the car the Bolivian national flags flapping in the breeze.

"Yes," Lucia said. She didn't need to elaborate. Then she turned to see downtown La Paz rush by outside their windows while Moberg looked at her appreciatively. She was born to this, he thought as he saw her beautiful hair and her aristocratic demeanor. It was late, almost midnight, but she could just as easily have been looking out over a crowd of her people, ready to give them a wave as practiced and as regal as any the Swedish royal family might have produced.

He leaned his head back against the seat and smiled to himself. I am making love to a new queen, or at least a first lady, he thought, happy with the idea. And why shouldn't he think that way? Her brother had the reigns of power, and he, Lennart Moberg, had the means to maintain it. The factory would go into production in a matter of a week or so, and from there, using his techniques, would flow an avalanche of the drug. The production of the drug utilized inexpensive and easily obtained chemicals and a highly complicated manufacturing system.

In a matter of a few months, using very basic marketing methods, they could have the new cocaine in the hands— and up the noses—of hundreds of thousands of new users. Even after an absurd markup on their end, the drug would be inexpensive enough that many more consumers would be willing to pay for it and become addicted. The profits would have been enormous even if they were to provide the amount of cocaine that was already being sent from Bolivia to the United States. But they intended to multiply that quantity now.

Since he'd come to Bolivia, Moberg had been reading the country's history, and he'd come across the stories of the life-styles of the tin barons who had been among the richest men in the world. That mineral had been a necessity for almost all other industrial products, and with the wealth derived from it, the barons had established a kind of life in La Paz that rivaled that of the richest oil sheikhs of the modern age.

That wealth was going to return to the Bolivian capital, and Moberg was going to be the one to bring it to them.

He looked over to Lucia and knew they would be in bed together soon. Her nails would be clawing his back, and her mouth would be biting his shoulders. He wouldn't care. Her actions would drive him to his own violent peak of passion, and he'd use it to subject her still once more—the way he always did in sex, the way she liked him to do.

Her act of being the queen of Bolivia was something he was happy to see her accomplish. Knowing what the supposedly regal and actually haughty woman would do for him—and to him—when they were alone, only made him desire her more.

The limousine sped through the gates of the presidential palace, and still another honor guard of soldiers in crisply pressed uniforms was waiting to welcome them with smart salutes.

They were home. They got out of the car and gave gracious, condescending smiles and waves to the men on duty for their sake as they walked up the stairway into the palace. They ignored the construction that was under way to repair the damage done to the old building during the most recent "troubles," as they were already being called, and swept up the staircase.

Although they never openly displayed their emotions in front of the staff, they did exchange conspiratorial smiles with each other. It would be only seconds before they got to their chambers where he could rip off her dress, exposing her beautiful body, then throw her roughly on the bed before savagely pouncing on her.

The last few moments that delayed their passion only made the taste of it when it finally came all the more sweet and wonderful.

VALDEZ WAS in the command post at the factory. There were times when a man like himself enjoyed being with his troops. The grandeur and glory of the soft life of the chief of state was already somewhat stale for him—especially since it meant staying under the same roof as the Swede.

Men of power who have risen up from the ranks liked it when they could make believe they still had touch with their roots. Even the Roman emperors would walk through the streets of Rome or the garrisons of the imperial army and playact at being common troops or merchantmen. They convinced themselves that everyone appreciated the gesture or that it was undetected, even though they would have a battalion of guards either shadowing them in back and front, eliminating any possible danger, or else themselves masquerading as commoners so they could deliver exactly the impression of loyalty and obedience that they knew the emperor would like to have.

Valdez was sitting playing cards with some members of the army detachment assigned to the factory. While he dealt and played his hands, he laughed and joked, finding great pleasure in the fact he was winning so much money from the poor troops. He didn't realize he was already falling victim to the worst self-deception of a ruler. After only a few weeks in power, he was already oblivious to the fact that the games were rigged in his favor and that the men weren't worried about losing because they'd been given a special allowance by the base commander.

Leadership like Valdez's isn't allowed to deal with reality very often. It's lulled into a false belief that all is well when, in fact, things are going very, very wrong. Advisers who should alert a chief of state to danger are instead intent on making him believe everything is going just the way he wished it were. There was no hint of anything wrong in Bolivia that night. The skies were bright and clean, and the stars looked diamondlike in the clear atmosphere.

All was well in Valdez's Bolivia.

15

"Our technical adviser," Claude Hayes said to Major Miscara as the pilot was about to climb aboard his F/A-18. "Mr. Sandow of Allied Studios."

"Señor," Miscara said, making a small bow to Geoff Bishop, who returned the gesture.

"Good-looking plane," Bishop stated as he stood back to take in the sharp lines of the jet fighter. "The U.S. Marines call it the Hornet, you know. This is going to work very well, no question. Of course, it'll have to be cleaned up before we can possibly film it."

"Cleaned?" Miscara looked at the plane and wondered what Sandow meant. "Well, not now, I'm afraid. The orders are very explicit that I must be in the sky in only fifteen minutes."

"Fifteen minutes!" Claude Hayes exclaimed. "Do you know how much fifteen minutes will cost if the stars are on the set? If the camera crews are..."

"If we do just a little cosmetic work on the markings right now," Geoff said, "it'll work for this setup."

Bishop moved to the truck O'Toole and Hayes had hired to move their "camera equipment" out of the airfield. O'Toole, supposedly helping, joined him. Hayes kept on haranguing Miscara with derisive comments about the lack of cooperation he was receiving from the air force, but he was also very gradually moving away from the pilot.

The three SOBs had made a survey of that isolated section of the field. There were only three guards armed with M-16s sitting around the base of the control building, idling away their boring nighttime duty. The building itself was manned with only a few technicians. Miscara, the pilot who was waiting to go up in the F/A-18, was armed only with a 9 mm pistol, something that was almost as much for show as for real fighting.

The SOBs knew better than to take anything for granted about an enemy. Making assumptions about the enemy's ability was the best way of getting killed, and they didn't expect that to happen to them if they could help it.

But it was going to be easy. It was Barrabas who would have the hard part tonight. Getting the jet fighter was going to be the simple exercise in the operation.

The containers that supposedly held the camera equipment were sitting on the bed of the van. Geoff and Liam opened its back doors and quickly reached inside the aluminum boxes. When they came back out, they weren't carrying video recorders, though. They had their own M-16s.

Their weapons had a great advantage over the ones the Bolivian guards were carrying, because theirs were firing as soon as they had turned around and aimed. The automatic rounds of the rifles spit a loud song over the asphalt runways. The three men who had been casually looking at them began to dance to the music, their feet moving more quickly than life as they carried them off to death.

The bullets from the M-16s sliced through the guards' chests and bellies, springing out small geysers of blood that soaked their khaki uniforms.

The bodies had barely settled on the ground before Liam and Geoff had both turned and hit the pilot. Miscara hadn't even gotten his pistol out of its shiny holster when the barrage of bullets cut through him and slammed him against the F/A-18's wheels.

The two SOBs ran back to where Claude Hayes had safely stood aside to give them a clear field of fire. Geoff threw his rifle at the black man, who was dragging the body of the Bolivian pilot away from the jet.

"Damned messy job, boys," Hayes said as he saw the deep red bloodstain on the rubber. "This'll never do for a feature release."

"Can the humor, Hayes," Geoff said as he tore Miscara's helmet off his unresisting head and put it on himself. "Get that damn control room before they understand what's really going on. I got to get this bird up in the sky and over to the factory."

"You got it," Hayes said. He and O'Toole ran across the short distance to the building. They got through the door unopposed, then jumped the stairs three at a time to get to the second floor where the air controllers were working. The door to the control room was locked.

"No time for the smooth moves," Hayes said to O'Toole. "Stand back."

Then Hayes pointed his M-16 at the lock and shot a short burst at the metal. The door burst open from the fury of the explosive assault.

The two SOBs charged into the room and found two Bolivians cringing in the corner, terrified by the outburst of violence they had seen and holding their hands over their ears to protect themselves against the horrendous noise.

But a third man was being a damned hero, screaming into the radio set in rapid-fire Spanish.

Claude turned his M-16 on the sucker, and the bullets ripped through the arm that was holding the receiver. The spray of bullets was so concentrated that it simply cut his elbow off from the rest of his body. His forearm dangled, held only by a few gristly white tendons.

The bullets had continued to fly behind him, and the windows had burst open, sending shattered shards of glass out onto the tarmac. Wind came in from the outside, a strangely fresh touch to the room that was filling up with the strange smell of blood and and a body reacting to fear and shock.

The veins began their pulsing of blood. The man watched with horror as his life fluids pumped out of him. "Get a goddamn tourniquet on him," Claude demanded. "I'd have just dropped him if I hadn't been worried about him falling over and ruining the equipment. Now you're letting him bleed all over the stuff. We might need that!"

"GENERAL VALDEZ!" a man screamed as he ran into the barracks where the leader of the country was still playing cards and drinking the local beer with his men. "There's something happening at the La Paz air force base. There was a broadcast from the control building, something about an attack being made, but I couldn't get a clear message and the transmission went dead."

Valdez looked up and tried to stifle the worry he felt. "Have you contacted the chief of the air force? He's one of my most loyal men. I made sure of that after the treachery of the asshole who helped Martinez slip away from me during the revolution."

"Yes, General. He says there's no information of anything wrong anywhere else. He had heard about the same transmission from his own people before I called. They insist there's nothing to worry about. But I . . ."

"But you're an old woman," Valdez said as he beerily looked at the smiling faces of his loyal troops there in the barracks. There was no cause for alarm. His men loved him! "You worry too much. If the air force says it has the situation under control, I'll believe them. Now, let a few men have a good time without all your craziness."

THE ARMY OF THE NIGHT moved through the fields on the outskirts of La Paz international airport. The guttersnipes of the city, they were dressed in the flashy clothes of pimps, in satin cloth highlighted with metallic threads; they were the lowlifes of the alleyways, men who choose their outfits to allow them to blend into the shadows of the city.

They had their weapons, mainly handguns of one sort or another—Berreta 9 mms were a favorite—and some had come up with some M-16s from the black market. In the background were four men—two pairs of two—who were working as the porters for Billy Two's own special armament.

There'd be some good talk over a lot of beers when their assignment was done with. Billy Two and Alex Nanos just knew there had to be a story behind the easy procurement of so many different things. Liam O'Toole and Claude Hayes were good, and they were dependable, but the ease with which they'd gotten the matériel was suspicious. Normal theft or bribery just couldn't explain their luck.

"Here, set that stuff up here," Billy Two ordered when they were about two hundred yards from the building that was their target. His workmen dragged their heavy loads to the place he'd indicated and gratefully left the crates on the ground.

"The rest of you, spread out. We're going to want attacks on all fronts. There are lots of guards in there with lots of new American rifles. They have machine guns set up, as well, on the roof, according to our information. As soon as I stop, you go in. But be ready. There's going to be a lot of flak coming from there unless my stuff works perfectly."

"Which it will," Alex Nanos said, "since you got your Hawk Spirit-thing with you."

"Alex," Billy Two said patiently, "we're going to have to have a nice pleasant conversation about that sometime later. I don't like the way you put 'thing' on the name of my spirit every time you bring him up."

"Let's go!" Pasquale said anxiously. "Please, you men can't be arguing this way now. We have a war to fight."

"Just a little raid to carry out, don't exaggerate," Alex Nanos said.

Billy Two frowned at the exchange and then knelt on the ground and began to use his knife to pry open the lids of the wooden cartons. In an age of computers and space exploration, he wondered what was going on that the United States government still hadn't come up with something better than pine boards to protect its armaments.

When the boxes were open, he dragged out a 120 mm mortar and set it up on its pedestal, aiming its line of fire in the direction of the warehouse. It was the finest and most reliable weapon of its sort the world had ever come up with. Easily transported, even more easily set up and used, the mortar delivered a high-impact round of artillery with accuracy so long as the range wasn't too great.

The range they had to take into account, a few hundred yards, wasn't bad at all. The Bolivians guarding the warehouse had been concerned with drawing attention to their activities and hadn't set up a defensive perimeter to include the outlying areas. Thinking their only danger could be coming from a direct attack on the building, they were lax about the approaches to it. They were worried about criminals, perhaps, but not an army.

They didn't know enough to be worried about the SOBs

Billy Two picked up one of the small missiles that was going to be the first salvo at the building. He could hold it in one hand. He studied the metal casing and smiled at the way the fins spread out from the cylinder at its base. They were like wings. Wings of a bird just like Hawk Spirit were going to fly through the night and deliver the deadly blow to his enemy.

Billy Two smiled, and the creasing of the skin on his face made his painted chevrons move like dangerous snakes shifting in their place. The Osage were ready to strike at their foe.

Billy Two placed the mortar missile over the opening to the barrel and then dropped it in. It slammed to the bottom, the action immediately igniting its explosive propulsive capsule. The mortar shot through the air, heading upward and then, after following a sharp arc upward, it began to fall toward the earth once more.

Baaammm!

The shell burst into flames as soon as it hit the warehouse. The flames lighted up the night, and Billy Two could see some of the guards trying to run away from the conflagration. He dropped another of the shells into the barrel. Since he knew that the range was right and that he was on target, he didn't hesitate, but kept on dropping the self propelling missiles into the machine, letting them all find their way toward their mark.

The element of surprise is often absolutely crucial in battle. It was a total success, judging by what Billy Two saw

The defenders weren't ready for the assault they were receiving. Many of them had been wounded by the mortars, and some began to rush from the building, a few even leaving their weapons behind. The criminals of La Paz were waiting for them. A hail of gunfire cut down those who were trying to escape.

Some were at least holding on to their dignity. One of the teams that was manning an M-60 began to shoot at the ragmuffin army that Pasquale had gotten together. Billy Two made adjustments in the aim of the mortar. He carefully dropped one of the missiles into the barrel. It soared into the air, as though lifted there by Hawk Spirit, and then crashed into the machine gunners.

The blast set off their ammunition supplies, and hundreds of rounds of the automatic's bullets began to explode in the night air, wildly sending deadly fire into the rooftop defenders.

From the distance the men looked like small dolls, jumping off the roof. Those who had survived the original attacks from the mortar were vainly trying to get away from this new menace.

Billy Two smiled grimly, then clenched his teeth and began to drop more and more mortars into the barrel. There was an aura about him that clearly warned he was best left alone.

"Stop! Stop the crazy man!" Pasquale insisted as he ran up to Alex Nanos. "He's blowing up the cocaine, all of it! The guards are all taken care of, either wounded or dead, or else we're capturing them. But he continues with his fire."

One after another the shells went on slamming into the warehouse, each setting off a new fire that was consuming the building and its valuable contents.

Billy Two ignored the pleas and the threats from the Bo livian. He was bent on eliminating the stuff, picturing being eaten alive by the flames.

The night was made for destruction, and Hawk Spirit wa hungry. On the rolls of the dead, new names were being en tered, and the name of General Valdez was among them.

NILE BARRABAS AND MANUEL stood in the small fishin boat and looked over at the factory on the shore. There wer some men working under lights, even at that late hour. Th illumination allowed Barrabas and Manuel to see the mor numerous soldiers who were standing guard over the site.

"I hope your people can come through, Colonel," Mar uel said. He looked back over the deck of the fishing cra and studied his own troops, a ragtag group of hearty mer but civilians, who were clutching a collection of antiquate rifles and pistols and, even in some cases, machetes an large ugly-looking knives that the men usually used to c open the bellies of their catch.

"My men always come through," Barrabas said wit complete conviction. "When they do, we'll begin our ow assault."

Manuel had stood beside Barrabas in the most viciou fighting in the jungles of Vietnam. He'd been willing to g up against a desperate enemy then, in order to join th American warrior in what they, at least, had thought was war for the protection of democracy. Now, they were t gether in Manuel's homeland. This time the meaning of th fight was much less ambiguous. They both knew the caus they were defending.

"There!" Barrabas announced as he pointed up at th sky. "There he comes!"

The jet fighter streaked through the night. Its swept-back wings cut through the clean Bolivian mountain air. Then dived toward the large industrial complex, after which its nose lifted sharply. Nile stared hard at the plane's trajectory and tried to imagine just where the bomb was, but he couldn't visualize it in the night air.

Barrabas waited patiently, then heard and saw the explosion as it ripped through the calm of Lake Titicaca. There would have to be at least another half-dozen runs at the installation before the—

But the one blast was suddenly multiplied in effect. The single loud *bam* turned into a rolling, crashing run of explosions as the entire plant seemed to be lost in an inferno unlike anything Barrabas had ever seen.

The fire swept outward like a hungry jaguar, reaching out with red and yellow claws to consume everything in its reach. Then, with an awesome roll, it turned in on itself.

"My God, Nile—" Manuel said with a hushed whisper once the sounds of the explosion receded enough. "Was that..."

The flames had balled up, then seemed to lift, still burning, rising in the air and leaving beneath them a column of fire that appeared to be holding up the circle of destruction.

A shock wave from the blast swept heated wind over the boats, and the men began to hurriedly cross themselves and to mutter prayers.

"No," Barrabas said, "it wasn't nuclear. It looks just like an A-bomb's fireball, but it wasn't that. The effect is caused by the extent of the explosion. It eats the oxygen from the air and then conflates back on itself.

"That one bomb, just one of the damned things, h
something highly explosive. It must have been in the chen
icals they were using.

"Your men are going to have an easy time, Manue
Nothing . . . and no one survived that blast. All we have
do is go in and clean up.

"Get the pilots to head for land. Warn your men not
try to fight the fire. Many chemical fires can't be exti
guished with water because it can actually help some of the
continue to grow.

"All they're going to have to do is clean up and make su
no one gets to the plant in time to salvage anything . . .
though anything could have survived."

Just then the F/A-18 swept down over the fishing fle
and dipped its wings at the Bolivians in greeting. The a
pearance of the sleek jet and its show of solidarity broug!
them back to thoughts of the future. Instead of their fe
and awe at the destruction they'd just witnessed, the m
were swept up in the joy of their victory. They cheere
madly, embracing one another and knowing that they
won.

They began to chant Manuel's name, and the soun
from all the boats rolled across the waters of the lake.

Manuel Negara looked at Nile, and there was no celebr
tion on his own face, only the knowledge shared by eve
warrior that simply because one battle was won it didn
mean others wouldn't have to follow.

THE SOUNDS OF GUNFIRE weren't loud when they fir
reached Lucia's chambers in the presidential palace. To h
ears they sounded tiny, and the little tiny *pings* at the cru
of the palace didn't convey to her any sense of real dange

But they were annoying. She got up and put on her
ressing gown and then walked to the window. Moberg was
n his stomach, naked, asleep after their torrid lovemak-
ag. She wondered vaguely about waking him up and hav-
ag sex once more. She rubbed a hand along one of her
rms, the one he'd used to hold her when he'd thrown her
gainst the bed at the beginning of their night. The mem-
ry excited her.

But she was distracted from those thoughts by the sight in
ront of the palace. There was a mob! The gunfire she'd
eard was an exchange between the dozens of unkempt men
n the streets and the guards who were protecting the pal-
ce.

"Lennart! Get up quickly!" Lucia said as she rushed
cross the room to wake him up. "They've come after us!"
he was shaking his shoulders, forcing him to become alert.

"What are you talking about?" the Swede demanded
eepily.

"There are rebels outside—they're trying to get into the
alace."

Moberg jumped from the bed and made his way to the
indow to look out at the gun battle that was going on in the
ourtyard. He could see a collection of civilians armed
ainly with hand guns coming toward the palace. The
uards were putting up a valiant fight, but already many of
lem were sprawled motionless on the ground.

"How can we escape?" he demanded.

"I don't know. My brother! He'll come and save us."
ucia seemed to be trying to convince herself of her
rother's omnipotence.

At first, Moberg though Lucia was probably right. Val-
ez would show up at any moment and the resistance would
e squelched. But Moberg suddenly saw something amid the

crowd of assailants making its way steadily in the directic of the doors of the palace.

It was one man in particular, whose face was painted wit extraordinary designs that made him look especially evil ar dangerous. At that very moment, the man looked upwar and actually seemed to smile at Moberg. The Swede w. startled and frozen in place, as though he'd been caught I the stare of the most dangerous predator he'd ever dreame of.

Then, as if by magic, the man's arms lifted up and the seemed to become claws! The talons reached upward in the night air, grasping in Moberg's direction. He started draw back from the window in fear. But it was too late as tl talons broke through the glass and grabbed him, tearin through his face, into his head, scratching out his brain ar ending his life....

"Lennart!" Lucia screamed as the bullet that kille Moberg exploded in his head. "Lennart!" she cried on more as she hurled herself toward his lifeless body. Just she did, another bullet crashed through the window, fin ing its mark in her skull, sending her reeling to meet a fin embrace with Moberg as Hawk Spirit joined them togeth for eternity.

16

Nile Barrabas stood on the edge of the crowd and watched as President Martinez was cheered on his return to his capital. The people seemed honestly joyful. They knew they were watching something unique in their nation's history: a victory of democracy.

Beside Martinez were Manuel Negara and his wife. Manuel was wearing a new uniform. He'd been made a general. Barrabas wondered if he knew anyone who deserved it so much as his friend.

Barrabas made his way alone through the throngs lining the last part of the parade route to the presidential palace. The rest of the team had gone on home, but he'd stayed behind by himself for that one special day.

Barrabas presented his embossed invitation to the guards at the palace and was waved through their security into the building. Even after having survived so many recent battles, the grandeur of the place remained intact, as though its solid walls would always be there, ready to house the best of the country if they would only allow it.

He worked through the dignitaries who were gathered and went up to Manuel. "A job well done, General!" Barrabas flashed a genuine smile at his friend.

"With good allies, there is no battle that can't be won."

A mere shaking of hands wouldn't have done justice to the emotions they were both feeling. They embraced in a gruff bear hug of honest affection and the greatest mutual respect.

"You've done something for my country in all this, Manuel. We've broken the back of the cocaine trade from Bolivia. A lot of young men and women in the United States are going to be clean because of this."

Manuel was suddenly much more somber and serious. "No, Nile. I wish I could tell you that it was true. But it's not. I have no intention of giving those people a free hand ever again—you can trust me. But in the poverty of our country, with the vast stretches of unpatrolled acreage in El Beni and the Chapare, it's impossible that the seduction of growing coca isn't going to return.

"We will do our part here in Bolivia, Nile, but this isn't the way you Americans can end the drug traffic. You have your responsibility, as well. So long as some of your celebrities and politicians and athletes and community leaders continue to show your young people that cocaine is something fashionable and desired, then the cost will be so high that the peasants of poor countries like ours will continue to produce it for you.

"It isn't just the source of the drug that contaminates America with cocaine, Barrabas, it's the demand for it and the prices people will pay that have just as big a part in making it flow from our country to yours.

"You have to stop the *use* of cocaine before we can stop the production. It's a partnership, Nile. We're all in this together."

Barrabas stood back and looked at Manuel Negara in his new, proud uniform, and he knew the man was right. Americans with all their money would always be able to get their drugs . . . so long as they asked for them. The answer wasn't in the jungles of Bolivia, but in the schoolrooms and streets of America's cities.

He saluted Manuel and smiled once more. "You've done your part, you're right. We'll find a way to do ours."

Then the band picked up, and the floor began to fill with dancers. The celebration had started, and the two men were forced apart by the flow of the crowd. Barrabas reached the entryway with long, easy strides, then turned to cast a last lingering glance for a war well done.

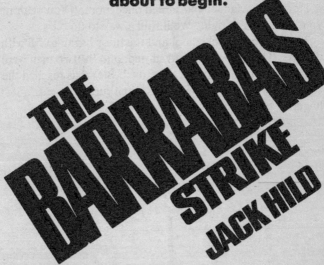

More than action adventure...
books written by the men who were there

VIETNAM: GROUND ZERO ™

ERIC HELM

Told through the eyes of an American Special Forces squad, an elite jungle fighting group of strike-and-hide specialists fight a dirty war half a world away from home.

These books cut close to the bone, telling it the way it really was.

"Vietnam at Ground Zero is where this book is written. The author has been there, and he knows. I salute him and I recommend this book to my friends."

—Don Pendleton
creator of *The Executioner*

"Helm writes in an evocative style that gives us Nam as it most likely was, without prettying up or undue bitterness."

—*Cedar Rapids Gazette*

"Eric Helm's Vietnam series embodies a literary standard of excellence. These books linger in the mind long after their reading."

—*Midwest Book Review*

Available wherever paperbacks are sold.

VIE-1

You don't know what **NONSTOP HIGH-VOLTAGE ACTION** is until you've read your **4 FREE GOLD EAGLE NOVELS**

LIMITED-TIME OFFER

Mail to Gold Eagle Reader Service®

In the U.S.
P.O. Box 1394
Buffalo, N.Y. 14240-1394

In Canada
P.O. Box 609
Fort Erie, Ont. L2A 5X3

YEAH! Rush me 4 free Gold Eagle novels and my free mystery bonus. Then send me 6 brand-new novels every other month as they come off the presses. Bill me at the low price of just $14.95 — an 11% saving off the retail price - plus 95¢ postage and handling per shipment. There is no minimum number of books I must buy. I can always return a shipment and cancel at any time. Even if I never buy another book from Gold Eagle, the 4 free novels and the mystery bonus are mine to keep forever.

166 BPM BP7F

Name _____ (PLEASE PRINT)

Address _____ Apt. No.

City _____ State/Prov. _____ Zip/Postal Code

Signature (If under 18, parent or guardian must sign)

This offer is limited to one order per household and not valid to present subscribers. Price is subject to change.

MYSTERY BONUS GIFT

HV-SUB-1C

TAKE 'EM NOW

FOLDING SUNGLASSES
FROM GOLD EAGLE

Mean up your act with these tough, street-smart shades. Practical, too, because they fold 3 times into a handy, zip-up polyurethane pouch that fits neatly into your pocket. Rugged metal frame. Scratch-resistant acrylic lenses. Best of all, they can be yours for only $6.99.
MAIL YOUR ORDER TODAY.

Send your name, address, and zip code, along with a check or money order for just $6.99 + .75¢ for postage and handling (for a total of $7.74) payable to Gold Eagle Reader Service. (New York and Iowa residents please add applicable sales tax.)

Remove from pouch...

unfold once...

unfold twice...

and they're ready to wear.

Gold Eagle Reader Service
901 Fuhrmann Blvd.
P.O. Box 1396
Buffalo, N.Y. 14240-1396

GES-1A

Offer not available in Canada.